HIDDEN WHEEL

by

Michael T. Fournier

THREE ROOMS PRESS

NEW YORK, NY

Hidden Wheel

Editor: Peter Carlaftes

Cover and Interior Design:
Kat Georges Design, New York, NY
katgeorges.com

First Edition

Printed in the United States of America

ISBN: 978-0-9835813-1-4

Text set in Goudy Oldstyle

Published by
Three Rooms Press, New York, NY
threeroomspress.com

"Barbarism lurks in the very concept of culture—as the concept of a fund of values which is considered independent not, indeed, of the production process in which these values originated, but in the one in which they survive. In this way they serve the apotheosis of the latter <word uncertain>, barbaric as it may be."

—Walter Benjamin

○ Introduction

Rhonda Barrett was an obscure but critically acclaimed 21st century artist. Her life was her work: she painted her biography, sixty words a day, over six giant canvases, before passing away in 2044. These paintings, including the partially completed, largely illegible work from her brief cohabitation with percussionist Bernard Reese, each measuring at least six hundred square feet, provide us with much of her biographical information (The Barrett Trust's aversion to providing passages for scholarly analysis gratis "in an effort to continue to raise funds for the betterment of young women everywhere" nonwithstanding). Barrett scholars agree on certain key points alluded to on her canvases—her early immersion in chess, her work in the sex service industry, her philanthropy, her subsequent rise to cult status—but the minutiae regarding her life was feared lost forever, as was so much of our digital archive, following the Great Flare five years ago.

The recent discovery of several boxes of paper artifacts belonging to Bernard Reese, experimental composer and Barrett's onetime lover, sheds new light on the life of the fascinating artist and her peer group. Among the effects found in a onetime bank vault in Chicago is what appears to be the beginning of a biography of Reese's former romantic interest, including extensive writing from his journals. I believe that Reese, who kept regular writing hours, began to edit these journal entries into a memoir.

In addition, sound recordings and transcriptions of interviews with Barrett's peers from the millennial Freedom Springs art and music scenes expose both the era and the relationships within it.

Dr. Rex Vineail, my esteemed colleague here at FSU, speculates that the vault's lead construction served as a protective barrier, saving audio media from destruction. That said, five microcassettes—fragile magnetic sound capture archives from the 20th century—did not survive the flare. Dr. Vineail was, however, particularly impressed that several compact discs—another 20th/21st century storage medium, read by a laser beam—did survive. Typically, compact discs began to slowly deteriorate once played. Those found in the box, from which I have transcribed many of the documents herein, remained pristine until recently, when Dr. Vineail and I were able not only to play them (with the aid of the FSU Heritage Museum's stock of early millennial sound equipment), but to save them to New Digital format.

I have attempted to reconstruct the world of Rhonda Barrett using the recently unearthed documents in conjunction with both her paintings and those precious documents which survived the Great Flare. I am particularly indebted to *ArtScene*, whose steadfast release of paper periodicals, even when the non-electronic publishing industry was left for dead in the 21st century, has proven to be predictive and visionary.

Historians and scholars who have worked on and around Barrett and her Freedom Springs peer group have traditionally done so in a linear format. The destruction of so much primary source material now renders attempts to do so virtually impossible. With no disrespect toward my colleagues, though, I must take this opportunity to say that the form never suited discussion of Early Millennial history. It is well-known that the advent and subsequent proliferation of hand-held internet devices bombarded Early Millennials with a constant (and then unprecedented) stream of information and advertising. In reading the recently discovered transcripts, presumably assembled by Reese, of discussions with Rhonda Barrett's chess mentors, we see a reflection of this glut of Early Millennial information. Rather than including full interviews from each chess player at Le Petit Chapeau, where Barrett honed her skills, Reese told Barrett's story as an "oral history"—a collage of distinct voices working together—allowing the players' viewpoints to combine and reveal details of Barrett's early life.

Similarly, we see the Early Millennial time period reflected in the voice of Max Caughin and his Urban Mosaicist paintings. Because Caughin's work no longer exists, his contributions to Freedom Springs' art scene have been largely overlooked. Through Reese's interview transcriptions, we gain a new empathy for Caughin, whose innovative work with, and on, digital and analog media unwittingly became a tragic performance art piece of the highest order.

To appreciate the Early Millennial era most, we must immerse ourselves in it. For this reason, I have chosen to tell the story of Barrett and her peers in a fashion that most reflects the era: unconnected yet cohesive, an Early Millennial Mosaic. The symphony of voices about and around Barrett provides critical context for her life, her work, and her love in ways which her paintings, in all their beauty, cannot. Where details were not available, I have taken small reconstructive liberties based on the scholarship, both extant and destroyed, of the best and brightest of my peers.

I hope that I have done justice to Rhonda Barrett, Maxwell Caughin, and the rest.

L. *William Molyneux*
Professor Emeritus, Early Millennial History
Freedom Springs University
29 January 2312

◯ Chapter One

LOU SCHWARTZ: The best player got the best table, closest to the door. All those nice pastry smells whenever someone came or went.

LUNA VALLEJO: The player at the end table had cars driving by, and the canopy didn't cover it. Some nights it was hard to see through the fog.

LEWIS BRINKMAN: Parents brought their kids, hoping they had the next Bobby Fischer on their hands.

RALPH O'KEEFE: It was usually me, down the end. I had to play those little shits. I hate kids, did I mention that?

LOU SCHWARTZ: I used to give Ralph such a hard time. 'The Demolisher,' that's what I called him.

LUNA VALLEJO: Ralph was the one who made the kids cry. I think he enjoyed it.

LOU SCHWARTZ: I used to ask him if he liked taking their ice cream, too.

RALPH O'KEEFE: Schwartz is a prick. You can tell him. I don't care.

SVEN GUNSEN: Movies about chess brought them, one or two a week. Magazine articles, less.

LEWIS BRINKMAN: I don't watch TV. I always knew they'd be coming when a chess movie was reviewed in the *Times*.

RALPH O'KEEFE: Brinkman didn't have to deal with any of it. None of the fucking kids. He was the best.

LUNA VALLEJO: The only one who ever beat Ralph was the girl. And she beat everybody, eventually, using Brinkman's lessons.

LOU SCHWARTZ: Ralph was so embarrassed to lose to her.

SVEN GUNSEN: I can't remember a child ever beating one of us until Rhonda came. Of course I felt bad for Ralph. But he was such a sore loser.

RALPH O'KEEFE: An eight-year-old girl beat me at chess. Of course I was mad. It didn't help that Schwartz was there, making fun of me.

LOU SCHWARTZ: 'The Demolished,' I called him.

LUNA VALLEJO: If [O'Keefe] had a sense of humor about it Schwartz would've stopped.

LOU SCHWARTZ: I knew it pissed him off, so I kept at it.

RALPH O'KEEFE: She asked me if I wanted to play again. I was livid.

LUNA VALLEJO: Ralph was caught by surprise that first game, so he slowed the pace. I could've told her it was coming.

SVEN GUNSEN: He didn't have the natural ability that some of us have. He learned by playing many, many games, rather than having something like we do.

LOU SCHWARTZ: He didn't have sight.

RALPH O'KEEFE: I was always good at counting games—bridge, whist. She started her attack on the fifth. So I started playing defensively on the sixth move of the second game.

LEWIS BRINKMAN: He aligned his pieces into defensive positions early in that game. And the little girl knew what he was doing.

LOU SCHWARTZ: I laughed so hard: "Is that the Grunfeld Defense, mister?"

RALPH O'KEEFE: I could've killed Schwartz. He doesn't know when to shut his mouth.

LUNA VALLEJO: She knew the defense he was using, but couldn't play through it. No one had ever told her how to attack a defense like that. My game is very strong against defenses. I never had a chance to talk to her about it.

STAN BARRETT: When we played at home, I followed the diagrams as best I could—it was the only way I could compete with her. She looked through the library books I brought home and memorized the position maps.

RALPH O'KEEFE: She was only eight. She got tired.

STAN BARRETT: I never offered her any real competition. I ran from her attacks for as long as I could.

RALPH O'KEEFE: Once she started to lose focus I went after her. I wasn't going to lose agin.

LOU SCHWARTZ: What a jerk, beating up on a little girl like that.

SVEN GUNSEN: He launched his offensive when her attention waned.

LOU SCHWARTZ: It was brutal. She cried.

STAN BARRETT: That was the first time she had ever lost.

RALPH O'KEEFE: She wasn't the first I made cry, I'll tell you that.

LEWIS BRINKMAN: When she said she wanted to play again through her tears I knew that we had something.

○ ○ ○

I GOT LUCKY HONESTLY IF the cop who gave me a ticket had any idea who I was he woulda hauled me in my shit is everywhere sketchbooks full plus the busted Dovestail shows I was just walking down to the Dingo to get a beer when he made me empty my pockets all he found was the marker I played it like I was new that night was two lampposts the guy bought it like I said he wasn't a graf cop because if he was he would've realized my style dragged me in instead of writing me some ticket for eighty-five bucks I paid in cash the next day[1]. Not that I minded it could've been a lot worse some guys go to jail but if it happens walking down to the Dingo it can happen when I've got my gasmask bag full of cans probably will only a matter of time starting to get the biz up off the ground old to be tagging anyway a young man's game so I was like all right next generation I mean everyone knows that even bad press is good if I got arrested it'd probably bump my street cred you know "local man on vandalism charges" noobs would be like whoa dude is legit but they should know anyway if they don't fuck them. I'm legit. Seriously fucking legit. The thing is that I had all this paint tons of nozzles what a waste to not use them. I could've given it away maybe left it down in the 'yard but it didn't feel right. I'd make the transition except canvas is expensive I can't get it under my shirt so big it was like what the hell am I gonna do next until this one night I'm out walking around after the Dingo I passed this construction site black tarps ziptied behind a chainlink made me wonder what was hiding I walked around until I found a hole looked in there was a foundation a bunch of trash nothing hiding except a big pile of wood. This is like a quarter of a mile from Dovestail that new corner gas station. The gate was shut but the chain was so loose I could squeeze through I went in dragged two sheets of plywood under the chain one at a time I was like no problem two sheets but the shit is heavy one and bulky two too wide to get a piece under my arm I looked around for a wheelbarrow but couldn't find one I tried to balance both pieces on my head like I was some third world woman bringing grain back to the village or whatever. I always wondered how they do that. But they were too heavy I had to leave one piece there put one on my head and started walking down neck killing me suffering for my art right around the corner a shopping cart I thought hey this might work I got the one piece in there at an angle it was fine enough room

for another I dragged the second piece back and got it in no problem
pushed the cart down the street the front left wheel wouldn't turn it
locked at an angle I had to push the cart to the right to make it go
straight. The fastest way back to Dovestail was down the main drag
but the fog wasn't that heavy besides it refracts streetlight worried they'd
see me with two pieces of plywood in a busted shopping cart they'd be
like this guy is shopping at the midnight lumber store bam! slap some
big charge on me search my place find the cans especially the sketchbooks which I burned by the way *you'll never catch me now copper* so I
took the back way. Nothing wrong with those places. You know some—
   Hey.
   What?
   This is, you know, for a book.
   Sorry. What was I talking about?
   The back way. With the, you know, shopping cart.
   Oh yeah. Sorry. *Bernie* knew some of those guys. You can edit this,
right?
   Right.
Bernie knew some of those guys before he started catalogues especially Amy she's been at that place for years even speaks it a little and
the ladies I hear the ladies are fucking dirty two three guys at a time
you name it. Crazy dirty. Damn. The blacktop was all chewed up
impossible no one ever even bikes down there it wasn't bad at first
pushing my shopping cart those people know how to party man just
got done with their shifts almost two in the morning right they're all
yelling playing music ba ba ba ba ba hey! I tried push down the road
fucking wheel pothole the wood like a sail for assholes I hear laughing
they start yelling stuff I don't know what they're saying thing is I don't
need to the words I know they're calling me a fuckhead or something
seriously if I had gone maybe one street behind the pavement would
be the same but at least there wouldn't be porches full of fucking
Brazilians on both sides just done with their restaurant shift laughing
yelling there's warehouse on the street behind on one side it wouldn't
be like stereo insults but I don't care I don't care I smile it's dark they
can't see me anyway probably just a silhouette through the fog I wave
instead like if I had a hat I'd take it off tip it for them they all laugh
some more the shopping cart keeps bucking to the left plywood I hear
clapping laughing the music ba ba ba ba ba hey! They're okay.

○ ○ ○

LYNCH ASKED BEN IF HE wanted to come along. That was how it started. Mostly because it sounded so unbelievable. He could've changed his name, if it bothered him, but it didn't. Not exactly. Getting things done was easier, but only among the gladhanders and turkeynecks in his father's circle. Regular people had no idea.

Artists had no idea.

Ben's gym bag, in the trunk, held five thousand dollars.

So they drove in shifts, that first time, slept, and drove some more. It was exactly as Lynch described it: a small line of cars at nine o'clock sharp. Each stopped at a black pickup truck blocking the road. A man in an USF cap stuck his head through the open window.

Open your trunk. Open your glove compartment. Get out of the car.

He recognizes me, Lynch said.

How can you tell?

He didn't point the rifle at me.

Lynch popped the trunk. They both stepped out. Two frowning men with rifles standing next to the pickup walked over as USF man patted them down. Ben's heart raced. Lynch had told him over and over again about it, how technically it was sovereign, the cops were paid off, vacuum sealed, the scent and warmth to calm you, completely safe. He smelled rifle oil as sweat trickled down his back.

Fine.

Get back in.

They did. Ben watched one of the riflemen deposit the gym bag in the pickup's cab. The other lifted a large box from the payload and walked, passenger side, to the rear of Lynch's car. The open trunk obscured Ben's vision. He heard a thump and felt the car bounce. Then a slam, and rearview vision returned.

The USF man held a white bag through the window. Ben took it. It was warm to his touch.

Go.

Lynch turned and drove away. The smell of fresh bread filled the car as Ben closed his window. Lynch had been right; it was calming. So much so that he almost forgot about the box in the trunk.

In the years since, the three maintained the same brisk tone, though Ben never again saw their rifles up close.

The boxes varied: IKEA, Target, Bed Bath And Beyond. Scentless, vacuum-sealed, maybe three times a year. Never quantity. Just enough to make connections. The perfect entrance to a new town.

○ ○ ○

IT HAD BEEN NINE DAYS.

I stood in front of the door with the passcode email printed on a sheet of computer paper. The email instructed me to punch five digits into the doorknob keypad, followed by the pound sign. So I did. I heard a click, and turned the knob.

Drab linoleum on the floor, scuffed, a fire extinguisher bolted to one wall. A brushed steel tank against one wall, plastered with 'hazardous' stickers.

I followed the hallway at the end of the room down to a small ledge in front of a sliding window. I whacked the 'ding for service' bell sitting on the ledge.

A woman rolled into view.

She pulled down her blue mask—she was Chinese, I think, maybe Korean—and asked if she could help me. I told her my name and appointment time. I was four minutes early.

She handed me a clipboard and pen.

There's a reception area down the hall, she said. Return this to me when you're finished.

I walked nine steps past the window, further down the hall. The reception area had a few chairs around a table roughly the size of a Frisbee, littered with sports and men's lifestyle magazines. A plant that felt fake to my touch[2] rested on a square table in the corner. The plant was surrounded with brochures. Good layout—whoever put it together had a nice eye for fonts and colors.

'When you make it big,' it read, 'we make it big.'

The first four and a half questionnaire pages were simple. I answered with checkmarks. No, I was not taking any medication. No to alcohol. No recreational drug use. I didn't think secondhand smoke from Amy counted. Yes, I attended a four-year college. No history of cancer in my family.

Then to the short answer section: life goals, aspirations.

I paused to consider my answer for 'life goals.' Making my living playing drums didn't seem like it'd work. But it was what I wanted.

And the best way to make such a living was to get a kit that didn't rattle with every snare hit. Which is why I applied.

My life goal, I wrote, is to become a professional percussionist.

The Asian lady was sitting at the window when I return. I handed her the clipboard, questionnaire and pen through the window.

I felt uncomfortable as she scanned my answers. My hand started to shake.

She spun the clipboard towards me and pointed with a fat finger.

This one, she said. I looked down. She was pointing at the alcohol question.

Not even at parties?

I shook my head. Not even at parties, I repeated.

She scanned the rest of my answers. You don't look like a drummer, she said.

I was wearing one of my pairs of grey workpants, and a white t-shirt I ironed the night before.

Maybe not, I said.

She put the clipboard into a standing file.

Okay. We'll call you. Probably two weeks.

Don't I have to—

She laughed. Maybe next time.

○ ○ ○

WHEN I SAW HIM PASS the window I wanted it right away. I slammed my laptop shut ran outside followed him down State to make sure if he went down to the river it was all mine I thought of showing up at parties everyone looking at me being like whoah Max! but there was chance this guy already got it it was his if he's not going to the river so I had to find out. I wanted him to walk through the intersection of State and Webster then cross Riverside to the pedestrian path[3] and river. It was the first day all year I left home without bringing a jacket or sweatshirt for later the fog lifted made it cold clear sunny wearing my orange reflector vest over a grey buttondown fluorescent yellow strips over my jeans. Since it was getting nice people thought biker which never happened in the winter. So I had to follow the guy. Blogging was important daily bread all that but being outside in the nice weather was good girls wearing shorts and haltertops walking down the sidewalk I would've missed some of them if I was still in the coffeehouse staring at a screen. The guy walking away me following him rod bobbing with each step checking out ladies.

Maddie walked up the sidewalk with a thirty rack of cans balanced on one shoulder. She's great and all but I didn't wanna lose my man I pushed over to the far side hoped that the thirty rack would block her view of me but it didn't work because she saw me off to the side was all hey Max wassup. Shit. She put the thirty down on the sidewalk which meant we had to talk for a few minutes which wasn't so bad but the guy kept walking down the sidewalk I didn't want to lose him but had to talk to Maddie for a minute. She said she'd been looking for my tags I said I had a run-in with this cop so I'm experimenting with new mediums prior arrests and shit she's like oh that's cool I asked if she was still doing courier work yeah she said I see Crank[4] a lot she didn't mention playing with Louis maybe because he was my roommate but probably because he was leaving Pee Valves it was supposed to be a secret he didn't get along with Eli any more Louis wanted more mathrock down the street the guy almost disappeared he wasn't walking that fast I thought should be able to catch up she said how's business I told her good that I was usually at Caffiend during the day drinking coffee blogging lots of clients people walking on the sidewalk I couldn't see him anymore if I lost him then I'd never know but the look was so good worth a try I thought about showing up at a party everyone being like Max, you look just like that guy over there how my perfect run would be over because I stopped to talk to Maddie. I told her I was late for an appointment she said oh okay I was just headed to practice anyway she smiled said goodbye maybe it's not a secret practice she said I started back down towards the river but couldn't help but turn my head backwards to check her out as she was picking up the thirty rack. Awesome ass.

The sidewalk was full of people more than usual it was so nice out faster to walk on the street. I sidewalked between two bumpers out to the road cars looked like they'd hit me I didn't think they would hoped not I had to pay attention to the people walking to see where he went. I jogged and jogged people must've thought I was a jogger at first but I was wearing jeans and a button-up I'd have to be a fucking stupid jogger to jog like that especially on a nice day. I passed parked cars one guy driving by honked his SUV at me normally I'd be like fuck off asshole but I was still looking at the sidewalk and jogged and jogged.

And there he was.

I stopped sweat on my back. I shinned between two parked cars like a hundred feet behind the guy again. I thought maybe he'd take either a left or a right onto Webster which might mean not the river terrible but maybe just a burrito or something I decided to follow him even if he did take a left or a right just to make sure. He didn't he stopped at the intersection pushed the walk signal button he crossed the street which I thought meant the river I hoped so I wondered where to get a vest and a hat like his. I hung back got a free weekly from the red paperbox chained to a lamppost flipped through didn't read a word waited for the little white man to light up he did. He crossed the street I did too.

Another block down to the river. The reflectors were for the winter before that it was Velcro but everyone jumped that train they always do with me pants with Velcro flies Velcro shirts especially Velcro shoes went up so much that it priced me out besides, I was there first anyway. Everyone knew it. Everyone knew I was first in Velcro. The reflectors weren't as good but I needed something else while I was waiting for inspiration to strike. Perfect in a way because the whole thing is accessories with the right hat box vest rod especially anything in the closet worked no overhaul except for ads shirts with ducks on them shit like that. Shorts okay for hot weather and then for the winter pants I wondered about the winter though because if there were all those things on the vest what are they called I can't remember the hooks might catch the inside of my jacket and tear it all up so I thought I'm going to need two vests summer and winter or move those things lures! lures to my hat. The white man lit when he got to the next intersection and he crossed I waited until it started blinking red before I crossed I didn't want to get too close then I crossed on the riverwalk really nice the grass mowed I smelled it he walked along the river me behind him. Joggers jogged by I like sportsbras a few gave me strange looks hopefully because I was reflecting not jogging.

He sat down next to a tree and put his rod down on the ground and opened his box and took out something I couldn't see because I was too far away put something on a hook probably worms or bugs I haven't fished since I was like eight cast into the river I was so happy he was fishing not just dressing like going fishing it meant I'd be the first guy to get that look and everyone would say Max has done it again. People forget I was first. I was the first fisherman I had it way before any of those other guys stole it from my shoot.

○ ○ ○

Ben thought JR's—thirty years of hamburger patties, cigarette burns on the wall carpeting, poles obstructing sight lines—was better suited to be a venue than The Kensington's tiny basement, with its pitiful (though box-fresh) PA system and newly paneled walls. Dingier was better, but neither place worked well.

The other option was the Dingo. It had the same gritty authenticity as JR's, minus the hamburger smell. None of the bar's patrons—a mix of artists and workers from the remaining mills—could remember the side room ever being used to put on shows.

Establishing that credential would matter in both the short- and long-term.

○ ○ ○

LEWIS BRINKMAN: Rhonda was a special case, obviously.

LUNA VALLEJO: I played at that coffeehouse for years. Never before did I see Brinkman take such an interest in a child. She spent almost no time with me.

SVEN GUNSEN: Brinkman was very by-the-book. Which is why we were surprised when he started playing with her.

RALPH O'KEEFE: I played them all first, usually. What a pervert.

LOU SCHWARTZ: Would a father knowingly put his daughter in a potentially harmful situation? I don't think so. But look how she turned out.

LEWIS BRINKMAN: I watched her play O'Keefe and Schwartz with great interest. Some of the moves she made early established her endgame. A fascinating mind.

LOU SCHWARTZ: She beat me the first time we played. Then I slowed it down, like O'Keefe did, and beat her.

LUNA VALLEJO: She didn't realize that her play had a predictable pattern. I could've told her.

LEWIS BRINKMAN: I began to play her every week.

RALPH O'KEEFE: The way he looked at her. Jeez.

LOU SCHWARTZ: I never saw it before, the fast track like that. Even Brinkman had to work his way up.

LUNA VALLEJO: Brinkman had been there since I started playing. There used to be a Japanese man before him, a retired conductor. I never met him, or played with him. Brinkman probably learned a lot from him.

SVEN GUNSEN: Brinkman told me he had taken the place of Takahashi. A composer.

LOU SCHWARTZ: (Brinkman) was always interested in the ways people saw the board. O'Keefe couldn't really see. He had a mathematical perspective. And me, I could only see a few moves ahead at a time. That's probably why everyone thinks she was so special. She had sight.

LEWIS BRINKMAN: Her endgame moves were sophisticated and far-spanning.

STAN BARRETT: She told me she could see the now and the later.

LEWIS BRINKMAN: It became obvious to me, as we played, that the depth and breadth of her vision had world-class potential.

STAN BARRETT: This was a man who had played a lot of chess.

LUNA VALLEJO: He had ranking before he retired.

LOU SCHWARTZ: It was all rumor before the internet.

RALPH O'KEEFE: I looked him up online. He was a great, great player. One of the hundred best in the world, at one point.

LEWIS BRINKMAN: I don't like to talk about my past.

SVEN GUNSEN: A humble man. There were stories underneath his exterior, but he never let those stories surface.

RHONDA BARRETT: His wife and daughter were killed in a car accident.

○ ○ ○

8:00 AM: Wake up. Push-ups, sit-ups, chin-ups. Masturbate (weekends only, upon acceptance).

8:30 AM: Shower, get dressed.

8:45 AM: Breakfast. Coffee (new or reheated), yogurt, granola.

9:00 AM: Journal.

9:30 AM: Work. Pamphlets, newsletters, catalogues.

Noon: Lunch. Hummus, pita, carrots, celery.

12:30 PM: Work. Pamphlets, newsletters, catalogues.

4:00 PM: Bike to practice space.

4:15 PM: Warmups

4:30 PM: Drums.

> *Band practice days:*
>
> 4:30 PM: Jam
>
> 5:00 PM: New Material
>
> 5:30 PM: Set run-through
>
> *Non-practice days:*
>
> 4:30 PM: Rudiments
>
> 5:30 PM: Set run-through

6:30 PM: Bike to apartment.

6:50 PM: Dinner. Fish or tofu, rice, steamed vegetables.

7:30 PM: Read. Philosophy, economics, criticism.

9:00 PM: Unscheduled free time: socializing, etc.

Midnight: Bed.

○ ○ ○

EVERYBODY HAD PHONES WHENEVER I took the bus anyplace people always talking ten different conversations when I'm on the bus I want to read a magazine people talking to each other are okay when I can hear both ends it's easy to blot them out with phones just the one side makes it worse can't tell when's next waiting for the other shoe impossible to read. At Dovestail we always had a landline[5] easier that way if you weren't home people couldn't get in touch with you besides everyone looked so fucking dumb walking around with phones but I held out. Everyone knows I held out the longest anyway. Then Louis got this girlfriend she called and called all the time like seven in the morning three in the morning six in the morning I asked him to shut the ringer off or maybe get a new girlfriend he got all mad and said she needs me this is after like two months right when Bernie moved out such a great roommate we never had any issues his dad though. Jesus I shouldn't be talking about this man I'm sorry.

No. Go on.

Are you sure?

Go on.

He was trying to streamline minimalize right when he started reading Ayn Rand playing drums said he wanted to get serious about being effective it was like okay good luck with that Louis he was a great roommate too real quiet which is funny because he always wandered back and forth on the stage stamping his feet like he was trying to bust through. Stomp stomp stomp. Stomp stomp stomp! Hey man what's wrong you look like something's bugging you did I say something?

I remember the stomping. Sorry. Keep going.

Anyway he said she needs me I need sleep I said I can't with the phone ringing all the time he said I love her I said maybe you should love her with the ringer off he got all mad then two days later he got a cell phone I'm not paying for the landline any more he said. I asked him how much it cost he told me it wasn't that different from having a landline just a few bucks more long distance was free a phone was too. A free phone! So I got my first phone for free a piece of shit that barely worked after I dropped it walking back from the Dingo when everyone else was on like their third or fourth phone so when I got my second one which wasn't too long ago I got one with a camera in it. I was like whoah there's a camera in my phone it makes sense when you think about it but in a lot of ways it makes none if I told the guy who was me when I was eighteen there was a camera in his phone he'd say maybe you can put a tape recorder[6] in your doorbell or something like that he'd be right.

○ ○ ○

THE DINGO CONCERT SERIES, A name he imagined before he booked a single band there, lasted one show.

Internet searches yielded the Pee Valves, a three piece alternating between feedback-drenched pop and complex songs which Ben thought willfully obtuse, and Stonecipher, a duo consisting of a girl on bass and a skinny bespectacled man in white behind the drums.

The Pee Valves headlined. Their bass player Louis' pacing stomps shook glasses on tables at the front of room, near the windows. They played all of two songs before a scuffle broke out in the back.

As time passed, the number of people who claimed to have been at the Dingo that evening swelled[7]: Max Caughin, who introduced himself to Ben before the show, had started the scuffle, planting two hands firmly on the press jockey who dared make fun of Max's carefully assembled vintage Velcro outfit and heaving with all his might. Said jockey, caught off-guard by the push, fell backwards, arms windmilling, onto the pool table, sending a shower of 'next game' quarters and half-empty pint glasses onto the battered woodtile floor. Max smelled like a huffer, but had too much energy. Was he on speed? Pills? Something didn't add up.

And Stonecipher!

They were terrible.

The drummer never played the beat, not once. And the bass player, the girl, pounded away at her strings with her fist, yelling into the microphone. The room's sound was awful—he was not asked to return; no big loss from an audience standpoint—so discerning lyrics was difficult. He wasn't sure there were any, so much as there were utterances sandwiched by growls: "mouthbreather" and "second and long" and "I'm not a people person." Songs began and ended seemingly on their own accord, with no structure discernable amidst the rumble. He had been mesmerized by the five or six fans in the front, fists raised, banging their heads to nothing.

The duo loaded their gear into the back of a battered Nova parked in the rear lot. He asked if they wanted to smoke.

I'm all set, the drummer in white said.

Day shift tomorrow, the girl said as she hipped her amp into the Nova's trunk. Thanks, though.

Ben produced a quarter from his khakis and handed it to her, along with fifty dollars.

What's this?

A sample, he said, of what's available. And your take of the door.

She opened and sniffed. What is this?

The particular varietal I have today has no name per se, as it is my standard. On occasion, however, gourmet mircobatches become available.

Amy opened the bag and inhaled deeply. This is standard?

Ben nodded.

Is this like a hundred grand an eighth?

Forty-five, Ben said. Eighty for a quarter.

That's cheap, Amy said.

Quantity, Ben replied. At any rate, thank you for playing the show this evening. I will be in touch regarding future performances. And please, don't hesitate to contact me.

○ ○ ○

(Excerpted from ArtScene *magazine/pulsestream 29.6, August 2037. Used with permission.[8])*

ARTSCENE: Your early history has been the subject of much scrutiny—

RHONDA BARRETT: It certainly has. (laughter)

AS: —but outside the confines of the chess community, I haven't seen much discussion of your particular vision.[9]

RB: The way I saw the board?

AS: Yes. Your mentor, Lewis Brinkman, has discussed your predictive chess ability in interviews, but in the course of doing research for this discussion today, I wasn't able to find anything from your perspective.

RB: My father brought home a combination checkers/chessboard when I was eight. Of course, I was thoroughly disinterested in checkers. To win, you don't move the pieces in the back, eliminating your opponent's ability to be kinged. It took me all of three games to figure it out.

AS: Did you have checkers sight?

RB: No.

AS: You were able to figure it out on your own?

RB: It's not hard.

AS: Of course. So, moving on, you began to play chess because you didn't like checkers?

RB: That's right. I liked the way the pieces looked—horses and castles and queens were far more appealing to me than stacks of same-looking chips.

AS: When did your sight first manifest itself?

RB: My very first game. My father explained how each piece moved, starting with the pawns. From then on, I could see a nexus of possibility attached to each one.

AS: Lewis Brinkman has used that word in past interviews, nexus.

RB: I didn't have the vocabulary to explain what I was seeing at first, so I described each nexus as a maybe-crash: Maybe the pieces would crash. Maybe not.

AS: That's not a bad description.

RB: As my father continued to explain all of the pieces and how they moved, each successive piece grew its own nexus.

AS: What did the chessboard look like once you knew how each piece moved?

RB: It was a glowing grid, full of possible trajectories and nexes. When I began to play, with my father, it wasn't hard for me to keep track of the game because Dad didn't have skills.

AS: He was not a worthy opponent.

RB: Exactly. He took books out of the library and learned openings, then showed them to me on the board. He was helpful in that way. He did the best he could, and I did learn names and strategies from him. But in a normal game I could beat him easily.

AS: Was he embarrassed?

RB: I don't remember him ever expressing any [embarrassment].

AS: How long did you play with your father?

RB: He and I worked on openings and endgames until I quit.

AS: Perhaps I should rephrase the question: how much time passed between your first game and introduction to Lewis Brinkman?

RB: Probably three months. I found out later that Dad—my father spent some time at Le Petit Chapeau before he brought me. He wanted to make sure the people could be trusted.

AS: Do you know what made him decide?

RB: There was a woman who played chess there when I started. Luna Vallejo. My father told me he thought people who played chess in front of coffeehouses were either hustlers or homeless. He was surprised that there was a woman there.

AS: Do you think of her as a role model?

RB: Why would I? I beat her.

○ ○ ○

AMY WAS NEVER LATE.

I agreed to move into Nine Northbrook to increase our efficiency. The little room in the basement packed with musty mattresses and filthy strips of old carpet wasn't being used (it was supposed to be a kissing booth at one of the parties when Amy first moved in, but the smell killed it). Moving eliminated practice space expenditures and cut my rent thirty-three percent. The only downside I anticipated was living with six other people. I decided the savings would be worth any hassle.

Didier went back to France, and I moved in. Most everyone was on Max time—waiters and bartenders. I was already on my lunchbreak when they woke up, except for Crank who got up at six to bike downtown for early messenger assignments. The house was usually empty when I went downstairs to the basement.

Amy and I were older than everyone who lived there by at least seven years. They weren't bad people, just young and new to the city. I did my best to stay uninvolved and out of everyone's way.

The door opened. It was Amy. Black streaks cut halfway down her cheeks. Her eyes were puffy.

I lifted my snare so I could get out from behind my kit.

Don't get out, she said. I'm fine.

I sat back down. Amy turned on her bass amp.

You think some broad is gonna make me cry?

I shrugged.

It's work. People were horrible today.

Today?

What else am I going to do? I fucked around as an undergrad, so I can't go back to school, and even if I could, I can't afford it, and I

don't even know what to go back to school for. I can start at some
other place and work shit shifts and make less money. There's nothing else for me to do.

I said nothing.

We need to keep practicing and tour.

I nodded. She's right, I thought. We need to get the first one under
our belt.

Can we play now or what?

Sure, I said.

○ ○ ○

THE TWO SHEETS OF PLYWOOD went fast I cut them into strips in the
basement eight one by four mixed spraypaint made a stencil it was
going to be the Fogtown Burrito logo but it was hard to cut out
wound up this twisted blob I gave away the first eight eight more in
the basement. What a waste of plywood. That shit hurt. I don't know
why I didn't practice convinced myself that it wouldn't look so bad
but it did what an idiot.

I got really bummed wanted to start tagging again didn't want to
get caught wasn't going to steal more plywood they'd eat me alive in
jail my friends all in bands banging away in practice rooms then in
front of people clapping yelling. I never got that. Web pages are cool
blogs but it's not the same so the Dingo regulars not really my friends
though all at practices but me took the same way home every night
mostly to have something to do the long way down by the river mist
coming off the water watching fog windows open over the ClearCola
building. The bad nights I walked all the way into downtown the
financial district miles abandoned mad how else would it end but
cops stupid shouldn't have waited so long to start twentysomething
writing on lampposts cans I'm too scared to use years waiting could
have been burning for real.

○ ○ ○

THE MASS EXODUS OF FREEDOM Springs' businesses left a district of warehouses vacant. In the course of his research, Ben discovered a failed venture into 'artist housing' by out-of-town entrepreneurs: the intention, he had read at the library, was to retrofit the former factories as lofts and live/work space. The developers' initial investment had been funded (and financed) chiefly on speculation, and conversion had fallen with the market. On his walks though the district, he saw decaying scaffolding and abandoned pallets of construction materials. Such obvious signs would work in his favor.

He settled on one of the smallest buildings: a former auto supply storefront. He signed a hastily assemble lease (that, too, he thought, would work in his favor), and began the process of renovation and repair.

○ ○ ○

STAN BARRETT: Brinkman was a genius.

SVEN GUNSEN: I've met many intelligent men. Brinkman was among the smartest.

LUNA VALLEJO: He taught her using us and took all the credit.

RALPH O'KEEFE: Brinkman knew our strengths and weaknesses. He never told her what they were. Or maybe he did, when they were finished. I wouldn't be surprised.

LEWIS BRINKMAN: I played her in the style of each opponent.

LOU SCHWARTZ: It was humbling, being dismantled by an eight year-old.

LEWIS BRINKMAN: The first game she won, against O'Keefe, was underestimation. He wasn't prepared, and her game, at that point, was based solely on overwhelming her opponent.

RALPH O'KEEFE: He took her for a while after (the first games). They must've talked about chess at least a little, because after a few weeks, she came back and could beat me almost every time.

LOU SCHWARTZ: I took it easy on (O'Keefe) after that because I knew I'd be next. He's got a temper on him.

RALPH O'KEEFE: Bullshit. (Schwartz) told me I'd lose my seat to a eight-year-old. He said I'd be the laughingstock of Freedom Springs' coffeehouse chess community.

LUNA VALLEJO: They both make up history to suit their needs. Brinkman told all of us that she would not take a table, ever. She was too young, he said. If he gave her a table, the focus would shift away from him.

SVEN GUNSEN: Losing to Rhonda made Ralph improve.

RALPH O'KEEFE: I got by on numbers until she beat me. There was always a chance I'd lose my table, no matter what (Brinkman) said. So I started studying. I wasn't gonna let that guy embarrass me like that.

LOU SCHWARTZ: Ralphie got a lot better. It was fear.

LUNA VALLEJO: Brinkman thought of my style as very predictable. I studied and played side games with Ralph.

SVEN GUNSEN: Luna was married.

LOU SCHWARTZ: I always wondered if anything happened between those two. Ralphie seemed more relaxed.

RHONDA BARRETT: It wasn't until I was in my teens—until Zaitsev—that I became aware of the interoffice politics of Le Petit Chapeau. By the time I found out I just didn't care any more. About any of it.

○ ○ ○

Bernard,

Thank you for your interest in CentralCryonics. *Please call our Freedom Springs office branch Monday through Friday between 9 am and 5 pm to schedule a follow-up appointment. We ask that you maintain the same regimen requested for your first visit.*

CentralCryonics

Sunday Matinee! February 26th @ 1 pm:

DEAD TREND

CRIMPSHRINE

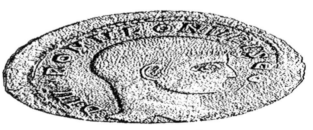

924 Gilman Street
All ages, no drugs/alcohol $5 with membership
Take the 9 bus from Berk. Bart

◯ Chapter Two

There was all that Louis broke up with the girl this is before Coxswain he dragged home this huge trashbag all points I said what's all this he said I don't know let's see so he went over to the stereo opened the bag and pulled out a disc cover like a rainbow with all this writing on it I couldn't read. These were in the dumpster in back of the video store he said the place the chinks went to he always said that chinks but liked them okay. Funny word to say. Chinks. Chinkschinkschinks. Haha. He put a disc in the CD player nothing happened hey dummy I said didn't you get those from the video store he put one in the DVD player[10] these dark words came onscreen after a title page filled themselves in with light we both got it the same time laughed Louis tried to sing along even though he didn't know the song can't read Korean we sat there watched them all scanned at least hoping for some porn but nothing most had like twenty songs[11] so after a few hours we had some favorites but not enough to save really just one or two for the next time there was a party and we wanted everyone to leave I guess Louis didn't want to throw them out so after I went to bed he took the bag down to the basement.

I lived at Dovestail for ten years found the place when I was moving to the city after college didn't know what else to do the landlords call it a coach house except it's hard to understand what they're saying their accents are so thick this little house three rooms kitchen bathroom basement which apparently is soundproof somehow even though they live in the main house like twenty feet away because man we have had some ragers Pee Valves played three or four times

25

Louis stomping around. Stomp stomp stomp! They never said anything we even had Bitchslap play once not a word from them nice people let us pay the rent like two weeks late give us weird vegetables from the garden no sunlight through the fog but they grew three-foot long squash no problem. Bernie used to have Stonecipher practices down there before he moved into Nine Northbrook with Amy and the rest of them to save money all these I guess they're called heads the things on the top of his drums like targets all the hits centered in clusters a broken kick pedal other drum gear from him a workbench stereo speakers TVs basically a giant pile of shit pushed into the corner so of course Louis is going to take the karaoke bag down there Dovestail's basement where stuff goes to die I noticed the bag while I was painting or trying to the other side of the plywood with my cans should've gone outside but if cops drove by they'd see me be like that guy must write graf then they'd realize who I was they'd search the place even though I burned the notebooks I must've missed something some practice board in the pile I'd get thrown in jail. I opened all the windows it didn't help much I still got pretty high was like whoah my foot kicked the plastic bag and there must have been a hole the disc cases came spilling out.

○ ○ ○

IT WAS ONLY A MATTER of time before people began making suggestions about the space.

In storage he had lumber, paint, and the PA he bought when Lounge Ax[12] closed.

He waited.

○ ○ ○

LEWIS BRINKMAN: O'Keefe and Schwartz were very good players. But Luna and Sven were exceptional.

LOU SCHWARTZ: I lost right away. Luna took longer. A year?

RALPH O'KEEFE: I have a hard time remembering dates. She seemed a lot bigger when she beat Luna. Her tits were getting big.

LUNA VALLEJO: I think it was around her twelfth birthday. I remember trying to talk to her about woman issues. She didn't want to talk to me.

LOU SCHWARTZ: Towards the end she'd try 'The Grand Slam': beat each of us, in order. Rubbing our faces in it. She was almost done with high school by the time she could get all the way up to Brinkman.

RALPH O'KEEFE: She did the Grand Slam a few times, before she quit. What a bitch. Thinking she was so much better than us.

RHONDA BARRETT: I didn't beat Brinkman until I was in high school.

LUNA VALLEJO: By the end, she took almost as long per game as Sven. I could've told her how to play fast and precise.

SVEN GUNSEN: When I learned to play, I found that I could see the possibilities unfold for each piece. My mind conjures up a film of the game being played and presents all the options, like a slow-motion shot in a sporting event. The options move quickly, but there are many.

LEWIS BRINKMAN: Her early games were fast, win or lose. I helped her develop strategies as she worked through O'Keefe and Schwartz. Her pacing was largely dependent on distinguishing the near future from the endgame.

SVEN GUNSEN: Each piece that she moved revealed more latent possibilities—what Brinkman referred to as nexus points. As a young girl, she did not have the patience to wade through all the options. Later, as he worked more closely with her, she developed separation techniques.

STAN BARRETT: Lewis told me to take her to the EyeWizard cart at the mall.

LEWIS BRINKMAN: EyeWizard posters appeared to be fields of visual noise. When looked at in a certain relaxed way, 3D images appeared from the mist.

STAN BARRETT: I thought the idea seemed silly, but we tried it.

LOU SCHWARTZ: Her game changed right away. She made sure to tell us all about it.

LEWIS BRINKMAN: The posters invite a certain relaxation of the eyes. Trying too hard to see what's hidden inside always yields the same negligible result.

STAN BARRETT: We went to the kiosk at the mall. Rhonda stared for ten or fifteen minutes, then started crying.

LEWIS BRINKMAN: She was staring at the posters. The trick is to stare through them.

RHONDA BARRETT: My father told me to pretend the poster wasn't there. I didn't understand what he meant.

STAN BARRETT: I told her to pretend the poster was a window.

LOU SCHWARTZ: The night they bought the poster they came back to Le Petit Chapeau. I wasn't there, thank God.

LEWIS BRINKMAN: It was past eight.

LUNA VALLEJO: All she could talk about was Mighty Ike.

RHONDA BARRETT: When I looked through the poster like it was a window I saw a smiling gorilla holding a banana floating in front of me.

LEWIS BRINKMAN: When she looked at the board in that same way, the near future and the later part of the game separated into two components.

LOU SCHWARTZ: I heard the game that night took forever. Her talking through the whole thing.

LEWIS BRINKMAN: She learned a new skill, and was happy about it, so she used it too often at first.

SVEN GUNSEN: The games took as long as mine did.

RHONDA BARRETT: Brinkman introduced a timer into our games. I used (the sight) less after that.

○ ○ ○

AFTER THE DINGO DEPRESSED WALKED down to the river mist mixing with fog buildings on the other side in and out of focus Louis called vibration in my pocket did I want to go out I'll be home in a while I said maybe we can sing Korean together he laughed hung up I stood there holding my phone. Clearings windows through fog bending the light mist haloes wait a minute I thought this is the next thing this and the bag in the basement.

○ ○ ○

I SQUEEZED BEHIND MY KIT.
THWACKzzzzzzzzzz.
THWACKzzzzzzzzzzzz.
THWACKzzzzzzzzzzzz.
It wasn't so bad.
Yes it was.
If we ever record the flaws will be evident, the way the snare rattles with each hit, the crack in my ride humming. But we have no plans to record any time soon. We can't afford it.
I couldn't concentrate during reading time. I walked down to Sheik. The kit I wanted was in the window.
My hand went to my nose, where the break healed badly.
I stood and looked in.

○ ○ ○

LEWIS BRINKMAN: She stopped playing for about six months when her mother died. Over the years I wondered what would take her away from us—learning to drive, maybe. Or sports. When she lost her mother I thought she was finished. We were all so happy to see her return.

LUNA VALLEJO: When she came back it seemed that she had aged ten years. I told her she could confide in me. She never did.

SVEN GUNSEN: She always looked tired.

LOU SCHWARTZ: She did a lot of growing during that time, too.

RALPH O'KEEFE: She filled out. Tits, ass.

LUNA VALLEJO: Rhonda used to turns heads when she played, but because she was little. That changed. I don't think she handled it well. I could've told her how to cope with the change better.

LOU SCHWARTZ: Her father stopped coming at just the wrong time.

STAN BARRETT: I thought she could use the space.

LEWIS BRINKMAN: She was always very determined, but when she returned there was an edge to her play that hadn't been there before.

RALPH O'KEEFE: She stopped talking so much when she played.

RHONDA BARRETT: I tried to use (chess) as therapy after my mother died. But it was becoming joyless.

○ ○ ○

STONECIPHER'S PALCORRAL PAGE BOASTED TWO horribly recorded songs and eight thousand hits. The traffic surprised Ben until he read the biographical information: Amy Czjdeki had been the bass player for Dead Trend during their reunion tour, eschewing the Buddhist rap-metal material of their last iteration in favor of their hardcore hits.

He listened to the demos over and over again, alternately intrigued and disgusted. The recordings were consistent with his live experience: growls punctuated by random utterances, a low bass rumble, sloppy drumming around the beat.

Pee Valves, their page said, split. He followed links to new pages and understood the schizophrenia of their Dingo show: half of the act had morphed into a lurching, off-time marathon playing songs about sharks and sailors. The other played straight-ahead pop celebrating summer and youth behind a wave of feedback. But both bands were playing at Kensington. Festival of Hamburgers, the pop band, were driving to Chicago after the show to record a demo.

Ben felt a bemused inevitability upon entering the Kensington's basement. The showgoers were largely the same people who had attended the Dingo Concert Series. He had been horribly mistaken in his move if this was all Freedom Springs had to offer[13].

He went outside.

Through the fog, he saw someone moving between lampposts. Ben became aware of a strong odor, like gasoline, which grew in intensity as the figure drew closer. The first recognizable feature to emerge from the mist was a torn jacket, pastel.

Max, Ben said. What's that smell?

Okay, Max said, smiling, you got me. He removed a giant marker from his pocket.

I didn't know you did graffiti.

Graffiti my ass, Max said. Mizst is an artist.

Can I ask Max something?

Max laughed. Sure.

Why don't more people come to these shows?

No publicity, Ben said. Katie's a great artist, and she does these flyers—have you seen them?

No.

Black-and-white ink drawings, like cartoons but fucked up. Anyway, she does those, but people aren't looking to lampposts for shows anymore. They're online, and no one in this town seems to care.

But you use lampposts.

Because no one else uses them, he said. Besides, they're advertisements for my walls.

There's PalCorral, Ben said.

Unless you're down with one of these bands you're never going to find out. Gotta write your name in as many places as you can so people know what to look for.

I wish there was a space dedicated to art, Ben said.

For serious. People could always go to one place instead of going from JR's to Kensington to the Dingo.

Ben and Max descended the stairs to the basement. Amy said 'check' into the microphone. Bernie hit the snare, fiddled with a knob on the side, hit, fiddled, hit, fiddled. Each hit yielded buzz.

Ben thought about Max, writing his name on lampposts.

Amy and Bernie finished their check.

We're Stonecipher, Amy said. This is Coxswain's first show. Festival of Hamburgers, too. And we're opening. Life's a bitch. Fucking GO!

Amy's bass grumbled under the no-beat thump of Bernie's drums. Secretaries, Amy shouted. Nurse's aides. Arglbl. Gah. GODDAMN ROLLERBLADES. Arggh. Beh!

A realization slowly dawned on Ben: they *practiced* this music. He recognized their mess as one of the online songs. Stonecipher had a trajectory somehow, a clear blueprint they followed, known perhaps only to them. Bernie, behind the kit, flailed away, dressed in all grey, looked up every few moments to grin at Amy, who turned towards the kit when she wasn't mumbling into the microphone. They must have amazing sex after shows, Ben thought, the way they communicate without speaking.

The thirty or so people at the show nodded their heads, trying to approximate where the beat might be. Could they hear something he couldn't? Feel something? Ben realized his interest in Stonecipher was half academic—how did they decide to do what they were doing? Why?—and half voyeuristic, like paying a few dollars to see the world's largest legged snake at a state fair. Being swindled was part of the fun. He wasn't sure if he was the legged snake, or if the band was.

He didn't think there was any money in them.

○ ○ ○

EVERY NIGHT AFTER THE DINGO I walked past the back of the video store to see if they dumped any more videos they did it was DVD cases[14] big black plastic I tried them they were okay but went into the basement pile practice I wanted everything to look the same. I didn't know if the DVD store would ever have the CD size again. Stupid. No one buys music any more or even keeps it. Downloads. I didn't want to wait to get more though so I just used what I had kept my eye open dumped the files onto my laptop blew them up to case size on the monitor the distortion of getting something so small so big made me see things different tried it out with cans first too hard couldn't control or get intricate got a brush from Leo Hamburgers at the art supply store. Ever use him?

Use him?

Leo's the sweet fucking hookup man hates his boss doesn't give a fuck just gives the shit away if you ever need anything he'll just give it to you.

I never did that.

What was I talking about?

Painting CD cases with a brush.

Right! I tried spraying and brush mixing didn't work wasn't meant for that I had to get tubes not cans went back I tried not to overdo it found two colors purple and this weird yellow I thought were good Leo told me to get more didn't whisper just said it get more I was like okay got two more he put a closed sign on his register the people in line behind me sighed grumbled said come on walked to the paint section threw like ten more tubes in my basket big tubes this is what you want he said. I was like what's so great about this stuff? Sateen DuraLuxe is a new brand of paint they sent us boxes and boxes of it to sell no one will even notice it's gone know what he said fuck it put all this stuff back and meet me in the alley so I did walked out through the front door people still standing in line at his register I was like haha! Suckers! I got the hookup! then around the building to the back the door opened he handed me bags and bags What are you working on he said I told him it was a secret he smiled said like your Faze tags I said shut up man you never know who's listening in an art supply store cops.

○ ○ ○

I AM TIRED OF BOOKS. I AM TIRED OF PEOPLE WHO WORK EXCLUSIVELY WITH AND IN THEIR HEADS. I NEED TO FIND WORK WHICH IS MORE PHYSICAL. I WILL DEVELOP ALL ASPECTS OF MYSELF: MIND, BODY, SOUL. I WILL NOT BE CONSUMED BY MACHINES. I WILL FIGHT. I WILL PROVIDE AN EXAMPLE THROUGH MY BEHAVIOR. SOMEHOW.[15]

○ ○ ○

THE SERVERS BECAME HIS MOST lucrative investment: everyone, no matter their vocation, needed to be online. He installed one hundred terabytes[16] of space in the room adjacent to his office. But he still dealt.

○ ○ ○

SVEN GUNSEN: As she grew, I waited for her to start talking about the latest pop bands she liked. That never happened.

LEWIS BRINKMAN: I asked her about music when she got to the right age—twelve or so. She had remarkably adult-sounding tastes.

RHONDA BARRETT: Rachmaninoff and Shostakovich were my favorites.

LUNA VALLEJO: She didn't seem to watch any sports on TV or listen to music. I follow music.

STAN BARRETT: Rhonda photocopied a picture of Baryshnikov from a newspaper and hung it on her wall. On a later trip, she photocopied Susan B. Anthony from a library book.

RALPH O'KEEFE: Thank God she never talked to us about music. It hasn't been the same since the Sixties.

LOU SCHWARTZ: She talked to us about the grandmaster matches. Those we were happy to talk to her about.

LEWIS BRINKMAN: She was fascinated by Zaitsev vs. Zoltov.

SVEN GUNSEN: Had the internet existed during that time, she might have watched the games unfold in real time. How good that would have been for her!

LUNA VALLEJO: She asked us about the coverage of previous tournaments. We all remembered Bobby Fischer. She was aghast that we didn't know any of the rest.

LEWIS BRINKMAN: She rooted for Zaitsev, of course. How could she not? He was innovative, young, attractive.

SVEN GUNSEN: Zoltov was us.

LOU SCHWARTZ: By then, she had beaten all of us but Brinkman. She just had him to beat, then she'd be on her merry way to beat businessmen senseless, or whatever it is she did. Or does.

LEWIS BRINKMAN: I lost my first game to her near the conclusion of that tournament.

RALPH O'KEEFE: We all knew it was coming. We just didn't know when. Personally, I couldn't wait. After all those years of diddling her, how would he react?

LUNA VALLEJO: I had never seen her so happy in her life.

LEWIS BRINKMAN: There were several games prior which I felt lucky to have won.

SVEN GUNSEN: I was happy for her.

LOU SCHWARTZ: I thought maybe she'd leave, finally.

LEWIS BRINKMAN: Of course I was happy. How could I not be? She was so gifted.

LUNA VALLEJO: After she beat Brinkman, she began to talk about playing Zaitsev.

LOU SCHWARTZ: The top of the heap at Le Petit Chapeau wasn't enough for her. Good riddance, then.

SVEN GUNSEN: She began to play in regional tournaments. She did quite well.

RALPH O'KEEFE: Suddenly she was gone.

LEWIS BRINKMAN: She still visited, of course, but it wasn't the same.

LUNA VALLEJO: I renewed my membership in the chess society so I could follow her in the newsletter standings.

LEWIS BRINKMAN: Her ranking rose steadily.

RALPH O'KEEFE: I missed her tits.

STAN BARRETT: She hung a photocopy of Zaitsev's face in her room and drew a target around it.

○ ○ ○

THEN IT WAS LIKE OKAY how do I do this tags people see my walls CD cases? No idea. Drill in the pile worked okay used to know someone at the hardware store from some Dovestail party maybe they weren't there no hookup I had to buy screws bolts did one hole at first in the center I started smashing the bolts at the end ruining thread they'd stay on the lamppost. People were taking them down which I hope is because they knew before everyone else that I was the man but I wanted people to see them different people every day. Then it was two holes top and bottom. Had to find spots ahead of time. Planning ahead and shit. Measured post screwholes in my notebook used to be full of tags just dots spaces. Not many river poles a few I found them took pictures blew em up did the work put it up. Those never got smashed or stolen. When I noticed I started looking for the poles first.

I thought that would be it find the best pole go from there but Ben told me—

How did you meet him?

Ben? I met him at the Dingo come on man you remember it was—

For the recorder.

Damn I talk it's like we're just having a conversation talking the good old days.

I know.

The Dingo there was one show there you guys sorry Stonecipher and Pee Valves before they split there was this guy there who gave me shit about my jacket so I punched a motherfucker in the face remember that during Pee Valves' set.

How did you meet Ben?

He tried to deal to me before the show said he liked my outfit except that guy he was always using those big words that shoulda been our tipoff but no one cared because he had Hidden Wheel and good shit if you were into it he must've thought I was because of my Velcro or something Louis Maddie Eli Katie shit Amy still smokes tons you ever smoke any of that?

Not since college. Did you?

I don't know he asked if I wanted to buy some weed I said no. Kids smoking weed to be like me all I need is a little coffee. Hahaha.

You were talking about Hidden Wheel before I stopped you.

Yeah Ben told me Hidden Wheel music and art I had to be the first artist plus a lady he knew. Serious street art he said represents the people but the people it represents don't always realize it something like that big words so yeah art show. My stuff on walls except hung there legal as much or little as you want he said of your past when you do it. I said I'll think about it in the back of my mind it's starting to get warm messengers starting to come out I had to get all the finishing touches on my new look look fresh for the opening. Find some fly.

○ ○ ○

I PUNCHED IN THE NEW passcode. Did they have a different four-digit number for every step of the process? I wondered if all the entries and exits were being downloaded to a mainframe somewhere.

No one was at the reception window when I arrived. Beyond the sliding glass pane was what looked to be the very corner of a huge space.

There was a gizmo that looked like a cross between a phone and a torture device on the left side of the window ledge—a series of tiny prongs next to a numeric keypad, and two metal flanges jutting out below. On the right was a black plastic three-ring binder which barely contained stacks of laminate. And the "ring for service bell." I obliged.

The overweight Asian appeared at the window. She sent me back to the waiting area.

I settled on a three month old news magazine. The plant in the corner, I decided, was probably fake.

A guy appeared, a few years younger than me, probably. An argyle sweatervest over an oxford shirt, and chinos creased severely enough to slice. Hair, heavy with product, that looked simultaneously well-groomed and messy, and the faintest hint of a flavor saver on his bottom lip (though he probably called it something different).

He introduced himself as Derek, and invited me into his office, maybe ten steps from the waiting room, directly across from the window. It was stark, aside from two—no, three—framed advertisements for the donation center: a smiling, attractive Asian couple, a black one, and a white one.

My paperwork had checked out fine, he said. I was pre-pre-quali-fied. The only thing left was to test my motility. He said he'd send me a date.

○ ○ ○

HE HAD KNOWN SHE WAS a painter for some time. At first, she was hesitant, which Ben found very professional; her pool, he guessed, was small.

Later, he realized her initial reluctance stemmed from the nature of her work: she had only one completed. When she talked about it, he was reminded of a little girl trying on her mother's clothes.

She continued to discuss her habits long after she had finished packing her valise and donning her long overcoat and sunglasses. She had just finished, she said, finally finished, and was waiting to begin her next.

Ben asked what she was waiting for.

It's not easy to find canvas as big as I need, she said.

He asked if the next one would also take seven years. She said she'd been overlong when she started, trying to fill it for the sake of filling it. Her attitude had changed.

Could he see?

She said she'd bring some Polaroids the next time.

Regular day and time?

He nodded.

○ ○ ○

LEWIS BRINKMAN: I have no frame of reference for how long it would've taken Rhonda to get to the top.

LUNA VALLEJO: I'd guess a lot of it would be political. She would've needed someone to help her negotiate the politics.

RALPH O'KEEFE: A hot little number like her? She had her own set of politics.

SVEN GUNSEN: In many ways, it seemed perfect. But we were biased.

LUNA VALLEJO: Whenever a new magazine came out I'd make myself wait to look at the standings.

LOU SCHWARTZ: She got what she wanted from us and then went for the big time.

SVEN GUNSEN: It seemed inevitable.

RALPH O'KEEFE: Fucked her way up the charts.

LOU SCHWARTZ: What she didn't count on was that computer.

LEWIS BRINKMAN: Zaitsev trounced the first MIT computer. Big Brain, it was called.

SVEN GUNSEN: Big Brain was a prototype.

LUNA VALLEJO: It didn't get much attention because it was the first chess computer.

RALPH O'KEEFE: And because Zaitsev beat the pants off of it. He was a prodigy.

LOU SCHWARTZ: There must've been some savvy PR people when they built the second one, Big Pink.

LEWIS BRINKMAN: The Big Pink tournament had national coverage.

SVEN GUNSEN: Some universities donated prize money. The winner—Zaitsev or the programmers—stood to win $20,000.

LOU SCHWARTZ: The first one, that Big Brain, calculated fifty thousand positions a second, and Zaitsev beat it. Big Pink? *Two million* positions.[17]

LUNA VALLEJO: We all watched the recaps.

RALPH O'KEEFE: Zaitsev started strong. He was kicking the shit out of that Big Pink.

LOU SCHWARTZ: After every game the programmers fed the computer data.

LEWIS BRINKMAN: Zaitsev's positions and moves were added to Big Pink's memory after each match.

RALPH O'KEEFE: Big Pink started to catch up.

LUNA VALLEJO: They played to a lot of draws.

LEWIS BRINKMAN: Zaitsev accused the programmers of cheating. If their computer was so smart, he said, it should be able to figure him out without help.

LUNA VALLEJO: (Zaitsev) sounded like sour grapes to me.

SVEN GUNSEN: It was a tremendous accomplishment for him to play such a computer to a draw.

RALPH O'KEEFE: How can a man keep up with two million positions a second? Even the best man won't see all that.

LUNA VALLEJO: Rhonda came more than usual during the Zaitsev tournaments.

LOU SCHWARTZ: Didn't have any friends, so she came back to us.

LEWIS BRINKMAN: She argued against the programmers. But there was an edge to her argument. It felt like she was staving off the inevitable.

○ ○ ○

—Hello, Jen?

—It's not Jen any more, Benjamin.

—Jennifer.

—It's Lara.

—Lara?

—Lara Fox-Turner.[18]

—What was the matter with your old name?

—You were one of the worst ones. Hit 'em like a ton of fish!

—I love that joke.

—Well, that joke is finished. It's Lara Fox-Turner now.

—How long has that been going on for?

—Since I started *ArtScene*.

—Funny you should mention that.

—Is that right? How are things in Freedom Springs? How's your, ahem, business?

—I'm starting my own gallery.

—Really.

—More of a show space than anything else, but there's some art.

—There are bands in Freedom Springs?

—Some. Have you heard of know Dead Trend?

—You can't be serious. The Buddhists?

—They were only Buddhist for a few years.

—They started the Zencore movement. People dancing around at shows wearing prayer robes, trying to attain enlightenment in the pit. A farce.

—But you know who they are.

—Sure.

—There's a band here with an ex-member. The bassist.

—Nate?

—No.

—Lou?

—Amy.

—Who?

—Amy.

—Was she early?

—She did the reunion tour.

—I didn't see them.

—They tried to set the record straight. They only played pre-Zencore songs.

—A relaunch.

—Maybe a reset.

—So there's an ex-member of Dead Trend in your town. That can't be why you're calling me.

—There are some other bands here, too. I've just discovered that one is on the verge of a distribution deal.

—What about the art, though?

—The most talented artist is named Rhonda. She's doing amazing work.

—What's it like?

—She has one canvas that she's been working on for seven years.

—Go on.

—She records her life on the canvas every day. Like a journal. She says that her work is a treatise against the Singularity[19].

—That's an interesting idea. What is her other work like?

—Her second painting is in progress. Exactly like the first.

—Wait. She only has two paintings?

—So far. She says it's her life's work.

—Interesting. But she probably won't sell.

—I haven't asked her.

—Artists like that never do.

—I wouldn't know.

—There has to be something else.

—The other one is this street artist. Calls himself Mizst.

—A tagger? I can't do anything with that.

—Not a tagger. A street artist. He takes pictures of cityscapes on his cel phone, and then paints them.

—Really. What's his medium?

—He uses CD cases.

—CD cases!

—He hangs them in the city, in view of whatever his subject is.

—Well, that's interesting. CD cases. Is he a musician?

—Not that I'm aware of.

—The commentary on dying media makes that interesting. Is he prolific?

—He is. He has a basement full of work.

—Cheap?

—He's never sold a painting before.

—So this diarist and the CD landscaper are going to be at your gallery opening?

—Yes. Plus the ex-Dead Trend band, the distribution band and one more. Coxswain, they're called. They sing about ship masts breaking, things of that nature.

—If I were you, I would get in on the ground floor of this.

—Oh, I will. And I'm going to release records.

—A record label! What gave you that idea?

—Records are cool.

—Same old Benjamin. Which band?

—Stonecipher. Ex-Dead Trend. Vinyl.

—Isn't the profit margin higher on CD's?

—Yes.

—Do you care?

—I'm not doing it for profit.

—Of course you're not. What's the date of the opening? We'll be there.

—We should meet at Fogtown Burrito.

—Fogtown? I don't ever want to set foot in that place again.[20]

—It's a martini bar now.

—Really.

○ ○ ○

I HAD NEVER BEEN INTERVIEWED in the newspaper before never played sports any of that stuff to tell you the truth I wasn't sure I wanted to be interviewed.

Bullshit. You loved it.

I mean I wanted the attention but once my name was out there all the cops would know where to come when there was new stuff hanging seemed like a dumb idea. But Ben said it would be okay in fact he said revealing my name would lend an air of respectability to my work or if I didn't want to I could not say anything which is what I did. I wanted to talk about being Faze but I killed him off already on CanDo letting the legend grow seemed like the best thing. If I went back out there did a bunch more Faze stuff actually did all the things I was talking about not only would I get caught maybe but it'd be all over the papers. People would laugh it might mess up the show it wasn't just me it was everyone all the bands I didn't want to screw it up the artist none of us knew yet.

So the reporter called asked all these questions about my work I told him that I was tired of tagging and Louis brought home this trashbag of Korean karaoke DVD's cheaper than shopping at the midnight lumber store. He asked me a bunch of questions about new media digital all that stuff I said man I like to support my friends. I don't really pay attention to any of that other stuff. Faze was a big influence on my work I said more than anyone else I mentioned everybody's band because those were the only names I could think of. Then when the article came out it made me sound really good like I knew what I was doing or something.

○ ○ ○

MAX FINISHED THREE CUPS OF coffee in the time it took me to drink mine.

I can't believe you didn't talk to them more about Faze, I said, pointing to the free weekly.

Faze is dead, he said, leaning forward in his leather chair.

What do you mean?

Everyone posted on CanDo—

What's that?

It's only like the biggest graffiti webpage there is. So I posted about his death on CanDo, the memorials came rolling out.

Everyone, huh?

All thirty-seven of me, he said, and laughed. He pointed to my coffee. Do you want a refill?

I shook my head. He walked to the counter to fill his cup.

When he got back, I asked if anyone had posted to the memorial thread besides himself.

That's the thing, he said. Writers came out, talked about how Faze was an inspiration. These big guys who didn't have the time of day for me when he was alive. Mizst should be easy. Everyone likes his stuff so far.

○ ○ ○

(From Freedom Spings Bugle, 7/19/2007. Used with permission.)

KEEPING IT ANALOGUE:
MIZST'S STREET QUEST
BY IAN DAXIAT

YOU'VE SEEN THEM, ALL OVER Fogtown: paintings of our skyline, blurry and primitive, capturing the essence of our cityscape. Or maybe you haven't seen them at all. The miniatures, painted on compact disc cases, disappear as quickly as their artist puts them up.

Keen observers have likely noticed a signature scratched into the bottom right-hand corner of the works: Mizst. The moniker is perfect. As we navigate Freedom Springs, the perpetual fog fades from our mind. If we don't think about it, it's gone. Mizst brings our atmospheric conditions back to the forefront of awareness. He reminds us that our city is full of beauty, despite the "armpit of America" tag that out-of-towners are all too eager to hang on us. The fog is a thing of beauty, especially at night by the river, where the artist's vision is presented with the greatest degree of clarity. If you don't take advantage of our city's evenings, you're losing out. You've missed it.

This weekend marks the grand opening of Hidden Wheel Art Gallery, the brainchild of Chicago transplant Benjamin Wilfork. "I had no plans to be a gallery owner when I first moved here," he said, "but I have been so impressed by the level of talent in the local art and music scenes that opening a non-profit DiY space to showcase them both seemed the right to do." The decision to highlight Mizst's work came easily for Wilfork: "He's the premiere artist in the city," Wilfork said.

Over the phone, Mizst sounds every bit the hyperactive coffee fiend his sheer prolifism denotes. His jovial tone belies the seriousness of his work. A onetime tagger, Mizst decided to shift his artistic output to compact disc paintings upon realizing that the music industry's grand plan of ten years prior had become outdated in the wake of file sharing. "Discs and disc cases were in the trash," he said, commenting on the wane of the onetime monopolistic juggernaut that was the music industry. "I wanted to use them for something." Indeed, the shiny discs which once meant so much to us are now regaled to the role of garbage. Instead of succumbing to the urge to rid himself of these relics of a now-bygone era, Mizst has transformed them into a reminder of our once-profligate consumerism.

Mizst reveals another twist: "I take pictures on my phone, then go home and paint them." The fog that envelops our city, seemingly ever-present, is reduced to a series of ones and zeros[21] in Mizst's low-res cel, before being fully brought to life with his provocative palletes. What was once a thing of missed beauty is rendered down to the barest essentials of our age before rebirth, using the detritus of the age which begat the rendering. His message: man will not surrender to machine, despite industry-driven urges to convert to a 'superior' product. The medium reinforces the message.

Mizst's modus operandi, also part of his medium, is localism. A firm supporter of local business—"I go to [coffee shop] Caffiend pretty much every day," he says—Mizst's work depicts a city whose artists inspire him to create his own. His favorite bands boast rhythm sections who pulse with the lifeblood of Freedom Springs. "Coxswain is great," he said. "Their drummer Maddie is the best. And [bass and drum duo] Stonecipher is pretty awesome."

Artistically, Mizst's work harkens back to the sophisticated scrawls of Faze, a renowned graffiti artist whose passing served as inspiration for Mizst to begin his one-man crusade to establish Freedom Springs as a viable artistic destination. "The z in my name is for Faze," Mizst said. "He was probably the greatest (graffiti) writer this city has ever seen. Without him, my work wouldn't be where it is today."

Mizst, and Hidden Wheel, promise to deliver a level of reliable sophistication to a city whose art scene has long been a punchline. Perhaps, with this visionary artist's help, we will discover that the punchline is the joke, just as he is helping us discover that the culmination of progress is merely the beginning of regression.

Hidden Wheel's grand opening, this Saturday from 9 to midnight, features an impressive roster of local bands: Festival of Hamburgers, recently signed to a major distribution deal; Coxswain; and Stonecipher, featuring Amy Czjdeki, onetime bass player of Dead Trend, Freedom Springs' greatest musical export. 137 Butler Avenue in Freedom Springs.

○ ○ ○

I GOT A MAJORITY OF my catalogues done yesterday before practice. The work for today will take an hour at most.

Amy called last night and asked if I wanted to meet at the Dingo. I walked over after dinner.

I had a sip of beer. I still like it. A lot. But I stopped.

Amy was with Seth, the first drummer of Dead Trend. I think they had three drummers overall—I know the story with their bass players better because Amy told me she was their sixth. I'll have to look it up. (Later: Three drummers, six bass players.)[22] Everyone always talks about how the early lineups were the best, before they started trying to play Zencore. I agree. The late stuff isn't all bad, though.

She first met Seth at Conforti's when she waited on him on his birthday, two weeks ago. From what she said, he was overjoyed that someone knew who he was. Then they bumped into each other at the supermarket last night and decided to have a beer.

He was a little chubby, kinda balding at the top, dressed normal. Thank God he wasn't one of those aging rock assholes who still think it's 1986.

Seth talked about how the Dingo used to be a lot rougher than it is nowadays. Most of the mills were still open, even in the late eighties. Aside from Dead Trend, there were maybe thirty punks. Every night they'd all cram into this tiny basement they called the Rat's Nest and drink cans of Venerable. He said they always wanted to put on shows down there, but he figured they'd get busted. I wanted to know where the place was, but he couldn't remember.

I had questions about where Dead Trend used to practice and where the early shows were. He couldn't remember those, either.

At one point Amy started making a chopping motion at her neck, but I kept throwing out questions. He asked if I was a journalist. I told him I was a drummer. He liked that. He tapped out the beats to some of the early stuff for me: Bad Policy, Defective Parts, Broken Bones, Maladjusted Youth.

Seth left at ten-thirty. He has an early morning job teaching troubled teens. I asked him if any of them were psyched to be hanging out with someone from Dead Trend. He shook his head and said none of them knew who he was. I couldn't believe it.

He said he had a good time, and that he'd keep in touch. He thought he might have some of his old show flyers at home in a shoebox. He said he'd make copies for me. I couldn't believe it.

We invited him to the art opening. I hope he comes. That guy has so much history in him.

○ ○ ○

THE MANAGER DISLIKES ME AND TRIES TO BURN ME OUT. CASES NEED TO BE RETURNED TO THE CELLAR, THEN BROUGHT BACK UPSTAIRS. HE SMIRKS. I MOVE THEM AND KEEP MY MOUTH SHUT. I HAVE NO FRIENDS THERE. IT WILL END AT SOME POINT. I CANNOT WAIT FOR THE NEXT PHASE TO BEGIN.[23]

○ ○ ○

I WENT TO CAFFIEND SAT there looked out the window one of those foggy days drank lots of coffee was mostly doing work but watched to see if anyone picked up the free weekly a few people did the name was right in there maybe they'd look to see if Mizst was too but no one really did I kept checking all day to see if anyone would and no one did that I saw.

I got five emails asking for help with papers so I wrote back all of them four kids from FSU one from some college I had never heard of before on the East Coast asked them to send twenty-five dollars to my eCoffers account one of them a girl did pretty much right away I sent her the word file with four lines of code I said paste your paper below the code then I sent her a separate email with the last line said paste this below the first four lines of code the file will go bad some of the kids that go to school have teachers professors I guess who are pretty fucking stupid not to pick up on an easy trick like that.

I am so confused.

Say you've got a paper due and you didn't do it or need more time or something like that you get in touch with me—

How do these kids know to get in touch with you?

They just do man I can't reveal all my secrets.

Okay.

Anyway get in touch with me and I'll send you the first four lines of code in one email then I'll send the fifth line in another you paste those lines of code in your paper and whoops! your paper is corrupted.

What do you mean, corrupted?

All the characters in the paper turn into boxes and asterisks and exclamation points shit like that a little minivirus in a file self-contained totally harmless then you get to go oops the file must've been corrupted and the teacher says just pass it in on Monday.

That's, you know, amazing.

I know, right? And all of the eCoffers money goes to an account in Dubai a dollar transaction fee and then that money goes to another eCoffers file for another dollar so it's twenty-three dollars all told but still easy money.[24]

Anyway I kept my email window open in case any of them wrote back two did right away while I was working on some of the blogs not a lot of work but it takes time to maintain all of them especially during slow periods when no one has anything coming out but I had to do me for a change. I never did me before. Not even Faze too much. So I made them all nice what you can do which is what I did still do is write like two short articles link twenty or thirty blogs to them if you rotate which page the content is on it looks legit and generates a lot of results then search aggregators take over from there thirty-seven becomes something like five hundred results. I had five pictures of Faze tags on my hard drive so I put those up linked to the free weekly and then went over to CanDo someone had already started a Faze thread from out of town I guess talking about what an influence he was so one of my accounts added links to the photoblog articles and I checked back on it all day and the page views went up from six hundred to over a thousand in a few hours people were digging Faze some people on the thread were calling Mizst a sellout motherfucker and all this and I just laughed.

All of the Mizst and Faze stuff took about half the day five cups of coffee then I was going to start doing Coxswain but I had a few more kids ask me for help with their papers so I had to wait on their money send it to Dubai and back by then some guy who was doing a movie about food wrote asked me if I could help him so I told him I could seventy-five dollars a day or a week for three hundred and he picked the week.

○ ○ ○

LEWIS BRINKMAN: A year or so later the same programmers built a new computer.

LUNA VALLEJO: Bigger Pink played Zaitsev shortly before Rhonda graduated high school.

RALPH O'KEEFE: She never brought any boys around to meet us. I started thinking she was some kind of dyke.

SVEN GUNSEN: She'd be away for six months, then visit three weeks in a row.

LUNA VALLEJO: The final match was on television.

LOU SCHWARTZ: She suggested we all go to a bar and watch it.

SVEN GUNSEN: She was eighteen.

LEWIS BRINKMAN: We all met her at a bar called the Dingo.

LUNA VALLEJO: (The Dingo) was a disgusting place. I could've suggested a nicer bar for her.

LOU SCHWARTZ: I almost choked when I walked in there, the stink was so bad. And I've been to some dives before.

SVEN GUNSEN: I had a beer. I could taste every other beer that had come out of the tap. I didn't finish it.

LOU SCHWARTZ: I remember Sven complaining about the way the beer tasted. He was not afraid of a beer, I'll say that about him.

RALPH O'KEEFE: I don't know how she got that place to play the match on TV. Actually, scratch that. I can probably guess.

LUNA VALLEJO: We weren't the only people there, either.

SVEN GUNSEN: Afternoon drunks filled the bar.

LEWIS BRINKMAN: The final match was televised at three in the afternoon on a lesser sports cable station.

SVEN GUNSEN: The table wobbled any time people put pressure on it.

LOU SCHWARTZ: Watching chess on television is awful. But we loved it.

RALPH O'KEEFE: The sound was off, and it didn't matter. The six of us sat and argued for the whole match.

LUNA VALLEJO: We tried to predict how the game would unfold.

RALPH O'KEEFE: Brinkman and Rhonda naturally adapted a lead man/color commentator relationship as they watched.

LOU SCHWARTZ: Some of the drunks gravitated to our table to listen.

LEWIS BRINKMAN: Zaitsev and Bigger Pink were even for many moves.

LUNA VALLEJO: I remember Rhonda reacting to a move Zaitsev made an hour in.

RALPH O'KEEFE: "That's it," she said. "It's all over."

LOU SCHWARTZ: "Bigger Pink needs to take the rook to start the endgame," Brinkman said.

SVEN GUNSEN: Of course, the computer took the rook.

LUNA VALLEJO: Rhonda put her head down on the table.

SVEN GUNSEN: I couldn't see as far ahead as they could.

LOU SCHWARTZ: It felt like those two were trying to put one over on us. We couldn't see the game ending.

LEWIS BRINKMAN: We both knew, Rhonda and I. We knew when he lost it.

RALPH O'KEEFE: Zaitsev looked like someone kicked him in the nuts.

LOU SCHWARTZ: Zaitsev lost. Just like they said. Showoffs.

LEWIS BRINKMAN: A day after the match, Zaitsev talked to the press about the inventiveness of Bigger Pink's moves. He insinuated that there were humans behind the computer's play.

LUNA VALLEJO: Zaitsev was sour grapes about that loss, too.

RALPH O'KEEFE: [Zaitsev] bitched to the press. He said he wanted a rematch. The programmers said no. Thank God. Can you imagine how miserable it would've been to see that guy get his ass kicked again?

LOU SCHWARTZ: That was the last time I saw Rhonda.

○ ○ ○

BEN KNEW, DESPITE ALL THE talk, that no one actually bought records any more. Downloading constituted theft, conventional wisdom said (and from starving artists, no less), but he knew everyone skulked home and stole whatever they needed once the conversation ended.

Shows were different. The most direct way to support bands, everyone agreed, was to purchase their wares directly in a live show setting. He saw it all the time in Chicago. And everyone always talked about it.

Vinyl was a key part of the equation. The shift from records to compact discs, in the eighties, had been genius from a business standpoint. After the failed eight-track experiment, people were wary of new technology. Better to buy a bunch of blank cassette tapes and dub friends' records than hand any more money over to an industry which obviously knew nothing about its customers' best interests.

But wait! the industry said. We're sorry about the mistakes that we've made. And to prove it, here is the ultimate in technology: a small disc which can hold twice as much music as a lowly vinyl record. You can listen to gorgeous digital sound in a portable device, or you can upgrade your home stereo and listen there. The music you love will be gorgeously clear, and devoid of pesky crackles and skips. Forever!

Everyone bought in. Slowly, at first, but then wholly. What a great run the industry had for twenty years! Especially considering the profit margins they pulled in: compact discs cost a dollar to make, but retailed at fifteen.

The collectors who brought up music's peaks and valleys being clipped by analog's conversion to digital were dismissed as kooks or Luddites.[25]

Small labels continued to release albums in limited quantities throughout.

Vinyl only, Ben knew, was best. Any compact discs he released would be online minutes after their purchase. It was easy enough for someone to rip a vinyl LP to digital, true, he didn't think scenesters would. Ripping LP's to MP3[26] seemed the realm of record collectors from the sixties who wanted to listen to obscure psych albums in their cars as they drove to work and mulled retirement.

Ben wasn't thinking solely of pragmatism when he considered vinyl. He was thinking of cache. Throughout the nineties, vinyl LP's were badges of honor, a third-party vote by in-the-know collectors and listeners who waited for vinyl's resurgence. And they, ultimately, were his audience. The thorny records he wanted to release would be puzzled over, blogged about, rediscovered in dusty bins twenty years later. His bands could sell them, enabling tokens of legitimacy, on one of their inevitable tours.

And he would lose money. Lots of it.

○ ○ ○

I SHOULD BE KEEPING BETTER records. Meeting Seth confirmed it. He can't remember where his band used to practice, or where he used to drink every night in a basement bar. It seems pathetic, being that fucked up all the time. But what if some of it's age? What if I start forgetting things as I get older? I need to do a better job.

○ ○ ○

I WENT OVER TO SEE Ben at Hidden Wheel brought all my stuff in two gym bags he got mad at me said the artwork needed to be maintained I was like chill out dude it's juts a bunch of paintings on CD cases which made him even madder. He yelled. It's art! Potential buyers will be here tonight Ben I said no one is going to want to buy my stuff a standard rate he said is fifty percent for the artist and fifty for the gallery we'll set each piece at three hundred dollars I laughed out loud how could I not I mean three hundred bucks for a crappy little CD case? He stuck his hand out said do we have a deal I was like sure Ben if any of these CD cases sell for three hundred dollars I'll give you half of the money. We shook hands. We fucking shook hands.

I took my drill out of the bag a few paintings in the other hand said here Ben where should I put these up he said you're not going to drill those but it was a question when he asked. I said I usually do no no no he said almost yelling again this isn't a lamppost this is an art gallery he took me into the back room all of the servers were back there humming away. He opened a toolbox on the workbench on the far end of the room safe underneath probably kept his weed in there and fished around inside for a minute his hand came out with a pair of wirecutters. Here he said. On the workbench sitting between paint cans he found a spool of copper wire instead of drilling through the work he said I thought that was funny work feed the copper wire through the holes on the sides of the CD cases and we'll hang them like so I nodded it made sense to do it like that because no one was going to come around looking to yank my stuff off the wall like a lamppost.

He asked me how I wanted to hang them what do you mean I said he said how will they be displayed I didn't know how many I had in the bags I knew it was a lot so I said maybe we can stretch them out so they take up a lot of space he liked that the ones that have similar colors I said can be together the ones that don't have a lot in common with the others can connect the like ones he started nodding his head that's a fine idea he said why would you do something like that? It makes sense I said to have like colors together no he said what could it mean besides that? I didn't know what he was talking about what could it mean meant a lot of little paintings didn't want to put them all in one big square but I told him that maybe it had something to do with the sun setting because I took a lot of the pictures on walks when the sun was setting he said try and find the brightest paintings put those up first then by the end of the exhibit he said hang the dark ones if anyone asks say that you're reflecting no ruminating on an era coming to a close that's cool I said which era he said which one do you think it is I thought about it for a minute all I could think about was Faze so I told him that he said that can be one of the eras but you have to think of more.

○ ○ ○

LOU SCHWARTZ: Of course we kept playing. She wasn't that big of a deal.

SVEN GUNSEN: She was at an age where we were going to lose her, one way or the other. Whether it was college or a job.

RALPH O'KEEFE: I never saw her after [the Dingo]. But I heard about her. And I wasn't surprised, believe me.

LEWIS BRINKMAN: The first time I saw her was in the financial district. My broker had been telling me to put money into search engines, so I went down to figure that out with him. And I almost bumped into her coming out of a building. I remember it was a nice day, and she was wearing a long tan raincoat, and her head was in a wrap. She had a case in her hand like a traveling salesman. I called out to her but she didn't look over. Her heels clacked on the sidewalk as she walked off into the fog. That struck me as odd. She was a tall girl.

I thought maybe I had made a mistake. But when I saw her at her opening, years later, I saw her hair. The headwrap made sense.

LUNA VALLEJO: I asked Brinkman so many questions to figure out what he missed. It was the case, I decided. There had to be something about the case. It didn't add up.

LEWIS BRINKMAN: Then the second time I saw her was at the opening. The article in the free weekly focused mostly on the other artist, Caughin—Rhonda's name was mentioned just once, at the end.

Aside from her hair, which had turned into long red ropes—dreadlocks, they're called—she looked normal. I was unsure what her reaction to me would be. But she was genuinely pleased I had come to see her. We talked for a long while.

I had to lean closely into her canvas to read what she had written. The characters were so small that from a distance her canvas looked like something else entirely, almost like pointillism. I was amazed by her level of precision.

She had started on her second canvas, she said, but it wasn't coming along as well as she would have liked.

When I asked what she was doing for work, she changed the subject almost immediately. Had I heard of multi-user dungeons?

I circled back to it later. She told me about delivering bread. Hanging on the wall was her painting, essentially a written account of her dominatrix job.

○ ○ ○

AS HE HOPED, FREEDOM SPRINGS' bureaucrats thought a non-profit gallery/show space in the largely abandoned warehouse district would encourage interest in the city as an alternate destination for artists and writers looking for like-minded peers. The permits passed through the city office in a matter of days, and at a much lower rate than the city's website had mentioned. No mention of the family history. Maybe they knew.

Ben put the occupancy and mixed use permits in the bottom drawer of his desk.

○ Chapter Three

Show tomorrow. Amy and I ran through the set three times tonight. We sounded great. I taped our rehearsal on my handheld. The sound quality is surprisingly good. I'm going to add the songs to the PalCorral page, so we have something up there besides those 4-track demos we did. The handheld stuff sounds more representative of where we're at.

Amy told me that Seth has called twice since the other night. I asked her if she told him. She laughed and said no. She's sure he'll come to the opening. We can introduce him around.

I hope Seth remembers to bring those flyers for me. Funny—six months ago I would've thought show flyers were nothing but clutter. I haven't had much interest in stuff since Dad. I could've kept his, but I couldn't see the point. Now I wonder if I was too hasty. Nothing I can do about it now except learn from it and do the best I can.

My appointment is Monday. Taking it easy.

○ ○ ○

(Excerpted from ArtScene *magazine/pulsestream 29.6, August 2037. Used with permission.)*

ARTSCENE: When did you first start sex work?

RHONDA BARRETT: I have never considered myself a sex worker.

AS: When did you start working as a dominiatrix?

RB: When I was twenty.

AS: What did you do for work before that?

RB: I worked at a bookstore. And I was a barback at a restaurant. I kept barbacking for a few years until I got enough clients.

AS: Typically, barbacking is a positioned filled by men.

RB: Sure. But I was tall, and in good shape, so I got the job.

AS: Was that the first time you got a job through your looks?

RB: I wouldn't say that the barbacking job was entirely based on looks any more than the bookstore job was. I was working forty hours a week and barely getting by at the bookstore—I had moved out of my dad's house by then. I figured I'd try working a job which was less mind-numbing and more lucrative. Plus, I didn't have to interact with customers directly.

AS: Quite a change from your later work.

RB: (laughter) Well, yes and no. On the one hand, I was working with them directly, obviously. But on the other, I was in a position, later, where I was clearly the boss. These men looked to me to provide a service, which meant I was in charge. The social agreement was much different than, say, waitressing, in which the customers are in control in a very obvious, sometimes oppressive manner.

AS: But your dominatrix customers were in control, were they not?

RB: To the extent that they were paying me. But I learned quickly that they wanted to lose control. Typically, these were men who were running Fortune 500 businesses. Their days were composed of bossing people around. There was no one telling them no, ever. After a point, being told yes all the time is harmful. So these men were technically in control, with their payment and their safe words, but beyond that anything was fair game.

AS: Are any of these men still alive?

RB: Oh, sure!

AS: Do you remain in touch with them?

RB: I get Christmas cards, little notes. They're very sweet.

○ ○ ○

BEFORE ANYONE GOT THERE WE all stood around waiting this painting was up huge like took up an entire wall looked abstract to me different colors blending together in patterns I guess I asked Ben who did it. He said it was Rhonda the woman I didn't know who she was he said the lady with red dreads the only girl I know who has dreads is that one who puked at Dovestail that time. The Puker. He told me it would change if I got closer so I did I walked up and it wasn't just colored patterns there were words in there but they were small I started to get a headache.

Ben was talking to the bands probably dealing his own place great spot for it I don't know why we're not headlining Eli said we have the distribution deal Stonecipher is the least accessible of the three. This is before he's famous too what a little bitch Ben said if they go on first what will happen to the crowd good point Eli said I didn't think of that still it's fucked up that they're headlining twenty minute sets Ben said starting at ten we'll let the art crowd have some time from there we'll let the show crowd come in.

The meeting broke up everyone wandered around looking at everything Maddie was following the art around the room I did it like Ben said all of the brightest ones were first a row of weird ones connecting to the next block that was when I had a lot of brown I wasn't crazy about it earth tone but that's what Leo had for me when I went to visit and so on down the line I think it looked good. Wow I had no idea you were such a good artist Maddie said she was wearing these pants that knocked me out hugging her ass. Awesome ass. Wow I said did you see my progression she laughed no I didn't know there was one I put my tacklebox down debuted it that night took her hand. She didn't seem to mind. Here I said let's go back to the beginning I led her over to where the brightest ones were look at this I said see how they're all the same color she said yeah I like the orange especially. I tried to remember what that reporter said what Ben told me this is the sunset of the era I said which one she said I said uh well pick one. She laughed you make it sound so mysterious like that. Is that good? She laughed again it's great now what about these she dragged me this time down to the brown ones I said well things are getting darker we went all the way down the line she kept laughing and dragging me when I said things got darker so I kept saying it I'd have to remember it for later if there were any more ladies.

○ ○ ○

IN HIS OFFICE, BEN OPENED a bottle of Nebbiolo with a bone-handled corkscrew. He could hear the lurch of Coxswain through the door:

We're going to need! A bigger boat! The hull is leaking! The ship won't float!

He put the corkscrew in his top drawer and left the wine bottle on his desk, next to three crystal glasses he brought from his condo.

Stepping outside, he saw a sea of heads trying to bob crowded around the stage. Behind, a couple in their fifties stood, squinting, in front of Rhonda's canvas. Another couple, dressed exclusively in battered denim, followed Max's paintings in their orbit around the gallery. The couple's man walked to the back corner of the room, where the first keg sat in a plastic trashcan. Ben had considered buying three kegs for the party, but then decided on two.

He walked closer to the stage, where the mass of crowd succeeded in bobbing their heads successfully:

Stem and stern! Cape of Hope! Humble spice! Periscope!

The engineer-boot-and-leather-jacket set, he thought, were patrons of the Dingo. The Kensington locals were the less hardscrabble of the bunch, with their Velcro track jackets and sneakers.

He wasn't sure about the homeboys.

He felt a pang of guilt at his suspicion. Maybe they were actively courting it: they slunk from cityscape to cityscape, enormous jeans sagging, looking left to right with each step in a manner that seemed to solicit trouble as much as avoid it. Ben stared, hard. They glared, then averted their glances. Sometimes the other way around.

Coxswain's song veered into waltz time, then changed to something resembling Dave Brubeck[27] before grinding to an abrupt halt. The crowd, Ben saw, stood, dazed, waiting for another shift in time and tone before realizing none was forthcoming. They clapped.

Benjamin Wilfork!

Ben turned away from the stage. Jen Fishton stood before him, long blonde hair Ben knew was dyed flowing from underneath a black beret. She removed a pair of sunglasses with one manicured hand and extended the other to Ben, who took it and kissed it.

Jen. You look great.

I told you. It's Lara Fox-Turner.

Of course.

Don't you forget it.

He smelled something. Gasoline, maybe. Coming from the street?

I have a bottle open for you in my office, he said. And three glasses, as you asked. The other two glasses are for—?

My personal assistants, she said.

Ben raised an eyebrow.

They're parking the Rover. Is this neighborhood safe? It looks abandoned.

It's safe.

Interesting crowd, she said. Some of the neighborhood toughs seemed in a hurry to leave. Does your gallery cater to trouble?

I don't know what you're talking about.

I was nearly knocked over by several hoodlums when I first arrived.

The homeboys, Ben thought. The smell.

Take a look at the art, Ben said. I'll be with you in a moment.

Ben walked to where he had last seen the thugs. On the wall, in fat black Magic Marker, next to Max's artist statement:

TOY

Ben peeled the artist statement off the wall and hung it over the scrawl. It wasn't a perfect cover, but it would do.

He walked to where Jen stood, in front of Rhonda's canvas. Very interesting work, she said. Is the artist here?

I haven't seen her, Ben said. He looked around the room. He had never seen her in street clothes before.

◯ ◯ ◯

AT FIRST WE WERE ALL like is anyone even going to come to this I started to get mad all that time spent writing bogus reviews for nothing at least I'd get to hang out with Maddie a little bit. That ass! But then some people started to trickle in it wasn't Crank or Cordelia it was people none of us had ever seen before like they walked in and everyone looked around kinda shrugged I don't know people we had never met.

Ben was there handing out programs my bio was in there he didn't ask me any questions for it just wrote it I guess I didn't know there was going to be a program one for the woman artist who hadn't shown up yet then bios for all the bands too Amy always gets mentioned as ex-Dead Trend or got I guess like she wasn't just the bass player on the reunion tour all hits they skipped the weird nine minute long Buddha prog-funk jams from their last album some critics say that shit is responsible for all that horrible rap-metal bullshit kids in malls listen to maybe they should do a tour and just play that stuff.

I went over to Ben to ask him how to act he smiled said it's going to be obvious who the artist here is I said what do you mean you're the guy who's wearing all black he smiled if people have questions I'll send them over to you. I wandered around a little bit talked to everyone I hadn't seen Ari for a while so we talked he introduced me to Lily who I already knew Bitchslap played the basement of Nine Northbrook that was like the third show at that house the cops showed up Didier our roommate who went back to France got dragged down to the station but he got off with a fine. The Burger asked Lily to be second guitarist Eli was only playing on about half of the songs now they were trying to have a frontman so they'd look more pro. They were both high as kites Ben doing his thing behind the scenes.

More people came in some of them were people I knew from going to parties and the Dingo the rest of them I had no idea about most of the people I didn't recognize were wandering around like the place was a museum standing back holding their chins nodding saying stuff to their wives or husbands because people like that who hold their chins always have wives or husbands pants tucked in brown belts loafers.

Three of them were doing the same thing with the chins except they were dressed the same not like loafers and brown belts I mean the same all black with turtlenecks. Turtlenecks! Well one guy had a mock turtleneck but still the woman who I admit was hot even though she was wearing a beret glasses long blonde hair kept leaning in saying stuff to the two guys in black except no berets they'd look at the wall then look around back to the wall the program around wall around. I saw Ben go over to them with a bottle of wine pour some into each of their glasses I was like wineglasses? Where did they get wineglasses at an art opening where the only thing to drink was a couple kegs of Venerable? But Ben poured wine into their glasses they held them by the stem talked nodded laughed they looked real comfortable together in their all black.

Amy came over bags under her eyes told me she liked my stuff had I seen Bernie. I told her no not all night. I kept looking at the turtlenecks wondering what their deal was Ben over there with a bottle he saw me looking waved me over so I went over there and he said I'd like you to meet some friends this is Lara Fox-Turner the editor-in-chief of *ArtScene* magazine I said hello stuck out my hand she looked at me I looked back she started laughing she said you've never heard of the magazine have you I said no never have the four of them were laughing usually when people are laughing at me I get real mad but it seemed like it was okay for me to laugh I did they seemed to like that I did too oh Benjamin the lady said I had never heard anyone call him that before these street artists are so charmingly something.

Something?

Yeah she was like you're so charmingly something. A word I don't really use. Begins with an 'n,' I think.

New?

No something that sounded French. If Didier was here I bet he could tell us what it was. I miss that guy.

Naïve?

Yeah! That's it! Street artists are so charmingly naïve so I said thanks they started laughing again but not mean laughing.

○ ○ ○

I HAVE NO IDEA WHERE to start.

Ben and Max did a great job hyping the show. Hidden Wheel was full all night, more than a hundred people there. Not just from the art supply and Dingo scenes, either: there were plenty none of us had ever seen before. Like the magazine people. (More on them in a second.)

Max surprised me. He's always talking about his work, in the same way he's always mentioning Faze and the web pages he maintains. Or so I thought. He surprised me by a) being a good painter, and b) having enough paintings for a whole exhibit. He says there's more in the basement of Dovestail, waiting for the next show.

He hung his paintings all around the room, a single row connecting a bunch of five-by-five groups. People weren't just there for the bands, like Amy thought. They stood and looked at Max's work, and Rhonda's, too. (More on her in a second, too.)

Coxswain killed it tonight, like they always do. People in the crowd I didn't recognize were going off during their set, despite time changes and false starts and everything.

The Burger didn't play well. Eli was wasted, talking from the stage about how they were going global with their new album, except he was so fucked up everyone thought he was saying 'going globo.' It sounded like he was promoting a blood drive. The rest of the band was pretty drunk, too, except for Ari, who kept perfect time, like always. I could see him getting frustrated back there, slowing down and speeding up to make the Burger sound better. Maybe Ben put them on second because he knew they'd get hammered.

We did well. I taped it on my handheld, but the playback sounds horrible. The usual happened: we started our set; everyone moved to the back of the room. Still, there were some people I didn't recognize up front, having a good time. There was this one woman, in particular, who was enjoying herself. I'd never seen her before.

When she came to talk to me, I wondered if she thought I was someone else. Women like her don't talk to me—the way she carries herself makes me think she has everything figured out. Plus, she's tall, and has high cheekbones.

She stuck a hand out for me to shake. I put it all together when she introduced herself. Ben told me earlier that the artist had dreads, and the only girl I know who has dreads is the one who threw up at that party that time. But she looks nothing like The Puker: Rhonda's dreads aren't mangy and unkempt like the ones trustafarians and hippies have. Hers are more like thick braids dyed bright red underneath a black head wrap. I bet they're not dreads at all, now that I think about it. She could probably undo the black leather cords around each and have normal hair.

Her painting was huge, covered with tiny writing which doesn't look like writing from far away. I had looked at it for a long time before the show, trying to figure out what was going on. It was like a journal—everything was dated on there, these little scraps of days. I asked her how many canvases she had. She was working on her second, she said. Each one took about ten years.

Ten years! I was surprised, at first. That's such a long time. But I wish I had started playing drums ten years ago.

I asked her how many she thought she might do. As many as I can before I die, she said. When she said that, her posture didn't change at all. Neither did her expression. She has a limited amount of time, she knows it, and she's filling it with work. I asked why she didn't do more paintings—smaller ones, maybe, like Max does— and she said that by using large canvases she will be able to empha-size her mortality. And by using such a large canvas, she said patterns might emerge.

Now that I'm writing this, I see that maybe people have a hard time with her. In a certain light, what she said can be seen as morbid. But I think it makes a lot of sense. To get work done, you have to have a regiment. She does. Next time I'll have to ask her about it. And why she does it. The scope of her work is so huge that it dis-tracted me from the reasons behind it.

I finished packing my drums as we talked. She asked how long I've been playing. A little less than two years, I said. She seemed sur-prised. How, she said, did you develop a style like that in two years? I told her I put a lot of time into it. Obviously, she said. But how did you decide to start?

I was about to tell her when the magazine people came up. Three of them, wearing all black, carrying wineglasses.

This woman handed us both business cards. She knew both of our names, and introduced herself as Lara Fox-Turner, the editor of *ArtScene* magazine (never heard of it). She launched into this spiel about how much she was impressed with the vibrancy of Freedom Springs's art and music scene. She went on about vitality and trends and timeliness and avant-garde, and the entire time Rhonda and I kept looking at each other. I was trying not to crack up. I think she was, too.[28]

So Lara Fox-Turner went on about the distinctive flavor of each regional scene, and told us that there'd be a profile of Freedom Springs in an upcoming issue of *ArtScene*. There will be a CD sampler included, she said, looking directly at me. Might Stonecipher be interested in contributing a few tracks?

Wow!

I told her that all we had was some low quality live recording. She said that studio-quality would be better. Maybe we could record before the issue went to print.

She told Rhonda that her work was impressive, too, and asked her to contribute.

I only have the one painting finished, she said, and it's not for sale.

Amy came over to tell me she was ready to load out. Lara Turtleneck introduced herself and started going on about Dead Trend being Freedom Springs' most valuable export. She had done her homework, I'll give her that. She mentioned the CD sampler again, which got Amy going. She's been looking for an excuse to record for a while. I'm ready whenever Amy is, except I need to get my new kit. And we have to pay for the session somehow.

Rhonda told me that a bunch of people were going out. She said she wanted to keep talking at the bar. I told her I'd meet her over there. She said okay, and smiled.

I can't believe I almost told her about the drums and Dad. We just met. This never happens.

We all watched her walk away. Who is that, Amy asked. I said that's Rhonda, the other artist. Amy kept watching her walk across the room. Bernie, she said, I didn't know you had it in you.

I didn't either, I said.

She's the most talented artist in your town, Lara Turtleneck said. It's a shame she has decided her oeuvre to be such large form. The market for fragmentary work is growing. But we should continue the discussion of your music.

Amy promised to record three songs for release, just like that. We wouldn't get paid, Lara Fox-Turner said, but she'd give us a hundred copies of the magazine to sell at shows. Her distribution was in the tens of thousands, she said. The Burger and Coxswain agreed to be on it, too, and she was trying to obtain the rights for songs from Bitchslap, Pee Valves, Weird Nuke and especially Dead Trend.

Amy laughed. Don't bother, she said. Those guys won't repress the records. They say that if you weren't there, you missed it.

We took our gear back to Nine Northbrook and unloaded. By the time we got to the Dingo, everyone had already left. We did see Seth there, though, so Amy had a few drinks with him. Two times this week I've been to a bar. I have to slow down.

○ ○ ○

THE FIRST THING YOU'LL NEED to do Lara Fox-Turner told me is get rid of the street name I said but it's in tribute to Faze she said I'm not familiar with his work he was the most influential graf guy Freedom Springs has ever seen I said she said that may well be the case but the artists who have most successfully crossed the bridge between street and mainstream success have used their Christian names. You may remember the short-lived craze in New York City in the early 80's I shook my head the only two artists remembered from that time are Haring and Basquiat both of them had their roots in the street but transcended those early roots partially because of their choice of monikers. I had to look those guys up when I got home I didn't know what their names were but I saw that guy Haring's stuff in commercials for sneakers condoms shit like that so I knew who he was the other guy had a movie made about him Bowie was in it that's the big time.

I was like who is this woman telling me what to do my first show tips on how to be a success but the magazine seemed like a big deal she was hot goth her two friends nodding about everything before that I had never seen a posse just heard about rappers having them Ben there with this weird half-smile on his face the whole time.

The look too is fabulous she said what was the inspiration? I told her I was sitting in Caffiend saw a guy walk by except he really was going down to the river to fish on a day with no fog she smiled god her teeth were white so you draw your inspiration from the seemingly mundane and incorporate it into your ethos I didn't quite get it but I nodded yeah that's right the seemingly everyday is really interesting to me. No. Wait. Intriguing. When I said that everyone nodded she gave Ben a look which maybe I wasn't supposed to see but it turns out I did. The ability to reinvent yourself is also important she said how long has this been your look I told her about the reflector strips the Velcro the gas station gear all that she nodded shot Ben another look very interesting she said. Do you foresee yourself undertaking any major projects soon I told her I felt like I was just hitting my stride with all the CD cases maybe I'd stop at some point but I liked what I was doing she nodded again said something else about the need to reinvent myself I nodded said I agree she said at the moment this is a very intriguing body of work she asked me if I had any more for some reason I lied to her. Oh yeah, I said. Yeah plenty of other stuff I was working on I thought of the trashbag of CD cases it was mostly empty I used a lot of them up but how hard could it be to find more that video store was always throwing stuff out I could figure out something else easy she said she'd like to see my other work I said of course of course.

○ ○ ○

A MAN IN A BLACK mock turtleneck whom Jen referred to as James drove the black Rover past a row of identical, abandoned factories and onto the highway. In the back, a man in a beret and black turtleneck sat mashed against the back door of the driver side. Ben sat in the middle, and Rhonda sat on the passenger side. Max leaned over the backseats from his perch in the cargo space, among bundles of magazines.

Rhonda, Jen said, we haven't heard much from you tonight.

You've been quiet so far, Max said, putting a hand on her shoulder. In a lower voice: I'd like to hear from you. Seriously. Why don't—

Max, right?

Yeah, he said. That's right. I don't know if you got a good look at my stuff, I mean my work, but by using—

Do you know those bands?

The ones that played tonight? Sure! Especially Stonecipher. Their drummer Bernie is my boy. I've known him since he moved to town.

He's pretty great, isn't he?

He is, Max said. Bernie. He's great.

The turtlenecked man in the backseat and Jen exchanged a glance and chuckled. Ben bit his lip.

Rhonda, Jen said from the front seat.

Yes.

Your work has such extraordinary focus. The level of detail is astounding. The brushstrokes! Immaculate in their precision! I've never seen such gorgeous and confident work before. I'd like to know what your plans are for the future.

My plan is to keep painting, Rhonda said.

To what end?

To the end of my life, Rhonda said. As many canvases as I can before I go.

Whoah, Max said, better not let her near the oven!

Jen nodded her head. Of course. But then, where does your painting go after you've died?

Come on, Max said. We just had a great time at the opening! We're driving around in a car talking about death now! Let's have fun!

I want it to be somewhere, so it can be seen.[29]

What you have may be a good start, Jen said. But you need more than a single painting. A portfolio. Perhaps you could shift your focus to some smaller pieces and return to your large work once you establish yourself a little. You are very talented.

It's not like that, Rhonda said.

What do you mean?

When I was growing up, Rhonda said, computers were a big deal. Everyone from our age group remembers the first family on the block who had one. Now, some people have two or three, or even spares lying around their workshops in pieces.

Intriguing, Jen said.

That's true, Ben said.

And you should know, Rhonda said. You have the room full of servers. How much memory do you have in those?

Terabytes, Ben said.

A unit of measurement which didn't exist fifteen years ago, Rhonda said.

Turn here, Jen said, gesturing to a freeway exit. The Rover cut through lanes of traffic to the offramp.

What's the next gradiation after a terabyte? We don't know now, but in ten years it'll be nothing. Terabyte flash drives.[30]

I'll have to upgrade, Ben said.

Take this left. It's three blocks down after the light.

I don't have any interest in that world. I'm glad people had a chance to see my work. I hope it reminds them that they're alive.

That's what good art does, Jen said.

So what's all this have to do with computers? Max said. I mean, Ben's got more space in that place than most companies do, so I think you're onto—

Has your system ever crashed?

My system?

Yes.

Start looking for parking, Jen said.

No. If it did, I'd lose all my pictures. And wouldn't be able to go to any of the messageboards. Do you go to messageboards? There's these people that go and post to them, bulletins and —

What would happen if everything was lost? All your pictures.

They'd be gone.

You didn't back them up?

I should. I never have, though.

James parallel parked the Rover.

It's like they didn't exist, Rhonda said. Right? If your hard drive crashes.

Unless I backed them up.

Which you didn't.

Right.

What's wrong with pictures? Remember dropping film off at the drugstore, and waiting a week for it to come back? How exciting it was to open the envelope?

I remember that, Jen said.

I am going to see how my work develops over time, Rhonda said.

Ben laughed. Let's continue this engaging discussion inside, shall we?

○ ○ ○

IN THE WAY BACK NO room to sit I leaned over and told Rhonda she looked good she smiled at me said thanks Lara Fox-Turner up front the little guy drove to Hub Seven didn't ask for directions rolled through the fog with no GPS[31] just knew. Lara Fox-Turner asked me what sort of work I was interested in I started to tell her about my PR firm but realized she was talking about my painting so I told her about Faze Nine Northbrook all the basement parties at Dovestail. She wanted to know who the most popular band was so I told her about Festival of Hamburgers she said they had attained a substantial advantage had a deal yeah I said distribution is it possible she said that a band of that stature would be willing to contribute songs to a collection I don't know I said I think so ask them do they have a lawyer she said jeez I don't know we never talked about it the other two bands she said the one playing off-kilter sea shanties and the duo I told her about Delilah and Louis putting an ad in the paper meeting Eli starting Pee Valves but those guys breaking up starting Coxswain with Maddie. She nodded asked the collection question again I told her I didn't know probably what of the duo she said so I told her about Bernie his crazy schedule drums cheaper than therapy he and Amy working at Conforti's getting shows because she played the reunion tour people like the name on the flyer. I told her they had a few songs up on their PalCorral page they recorded themselves with a four-track but never went to a studio or put out a record interesting she said.

She asked you all that?

Yeah she asked about everyone.

○ ○ ○

AFTER A CERTAIN POINT, PARTAKING wasn't necessary, not with the amount of documentation and discussion available. In Chicago, by the end, he led entire conversations in which he was certain the person to whom he spoke didn't have the faintest idea what recondite bands and artists he was discussing, but feigned interest and knowledge regardless. At first he thought such conversations were simply a tacit social agreement by two parties to engage in a kind of smalltalk which revolved around gossip and hearsay. But it became clear, as his stack of index cards grew, that the shorthand he developed for himself was largely without peer, save for the knowledge held and shared by the people of the era. Even then, drugs and alcohol muddled perceptions. He expected they would continue to do so.

○ ○ ○

HE IS ALWAYS THERE, IN FRONT OF THE MARKET, UNTIL THEY SHOO HIM AWAY. HE SMELLS LIKE CESSPOOLS. ALWAYS THE SAME CLOTHES. HE IS THIN. HE LOOKS HUNGRY. I FEEL SORRY FOR HIM. I GO IN TO BUY MY FRESH GREENS AND ASAIN NOODLES. I GIVE HIM TWENTY DOLLARS EVERY TIME I SEE HIM. I TELL HIM TO BUY FOOD.

○ ○ ○

SO THASS IT, BASICALLY, MAX said. That's why Faze's work was such an influence on me. He might not be that well-known, but you just wait. He will be.

Of course, Jen said. The market is beginning to correct itself to take street art into account.

The CD cases, Ben said.

Right! Right. You see, CD's being media which are getting phased out, right, in favor of MP3's and all. What if your laptop crashes? Your whole music collection will be gone, just like that. So you have to—

Unless you've backed it up, Rhonda said.

What?

Unless you've backed it up.

Backed up your entire music collection? You know how much space that would take? You were talking about terabytes before. Jeez, if I was—

By not backing everything up, you're making your music more disposable, Rhonda said. You have to get it all again. You're perpetuating it.

I don't have the space to back everything up. My collection is huge.

Do you have any records?

Like vinyl?

Yes, Rhonda said.

I used to. But then I converted everything to digital.

Why did you do that?

It's easier, Max said. I can bring my whole collection anywhere.

Why would you want to bring a whole collection of anything anywhere?

Because I can, Max said. And what if I need something?

I suppose, Rhonda said.

You don't agree, Jen said.

No, Rhonda said. I don't. I think Ben has the right idea. People should gather.

I can play any of the records on my hard drive for the whole community, Max said.

It's not the same, Rhonda said, pushing her untouched gin and tonic to the center of the table. Ms. Fox-Turner, it was nice to meet you. Ben, thank you for everything.

Sure, he said. Regular time?

She glared at him.

Nice talking to you, Max, Rhonda said. Tell Bernie I said hello. He should call me.

Max waved at her. He turned to the men wearing black. She's a tough chick, he said. Reminds me of this girl I went to school with who used to hang from hooks on the ceiling. You should've seen the ink on her!

Max, Jen said, are you at all familiar with urban mosaicism?

Gotta go take a piss, he said, standing. I'll be right back.

Your Rhonda, Jen said, is intriguing.

She certainly is.

I'm amazed by her long-term vision. By the time she is ready to sell her first work, there will be a bidding war following years of exhibits and hype.

She has a mission.

She certainly does. Not many artists can so seamlessly meld trajectory with ideology. Her anti-technology stance adds legitimacy to her work. It's brilliant. Seldom do such young, raw artists have their concepts so well-thought.

○ ○ ○

I COULDN'T BELIEVE HUB SEVEN used to be Fogtown all of the mustard colored walls were gone exposed brick dark wood instead Lara Fox-Turner ordered drink after drink told me her expense account would take care of everything her posse laughed laughed drinks kept coming fancy ones in tall martini glasses with names I had never heard before Lara Fox-Turner went on and on about the authenticity of the place the bartender chipped his own ice I guess used those little measuring shot glasses to get every drink the same there is a consistency she said which is admirable. Consistency is a large part of the game Maxwell she told me pushing another dark drink toward me I was fucking hammered but kept drinking anyway free booze what are you going to do.

I don't want this to get around she said but *ArtScene* will be running a full-color pictorial of the exhibit tonight in our next issue that's great I said my drink tasted like licking a pine tree I'm really excited for everyone the other artist is intriguing but apparently her work is not for sale which means that you Maxwell will be the subject of much attention when the article hits the stand wow I said I can't wait she said you should be prepared for the furor your work will cause people will be so excited that you have more paintings ready you mentioned earlier that you have many more ready I didn't remember saying that but I nodded yeah I'm always painting it is good to be one step ahead of the game she said she touched the collar of my fishing vest it is always good to reinvent yourself. Thinking ahead is the best thing you can do okay I said.

○ ○ ○

(Interview with Lara Fox-Turner: "My *ArtScene* Life." *Time* magazine/
pulsestream, April 7, 2041. Used with permission.)

TIME: What will you do when you retire?

LARA FOX-TURNER: I'll be doing a lot of the same things I have
always done: attend art shows, openings, rock shows.

T: Rock shows?

L F-T: Forever young. (laughter) And I'll have more time to read
books. Much more time to spoil my grandchildren rotten.

T: *ArtScene* started off as a sixteen-page magazine. Did you ever
have any inkling that you'd be so successful?

L F-T: The original concept—to travel to different cities, and document their art and music scenes—seemed the best job in the world.
When I got the magazine running, with the help of my investors, we
traveled and documented art that we loved and thought important.
To us, that was success. Everything else was extra. I have been blessed
to make a living this way.

T: What would you consider your proudest moment?

L F-T: I'm certainly proud of the way pulsestream technology has
revolutionized periodicals and books. To have the chance to work on
an efficient, environmentally conscious method of information delivery
which has helped alleviate problems of pollution and deforestation is
my proudest accomplishment.

My proudest moment, in terms of the magazine, isn't a moment per
se, but a discovery. My dear friend Benjamin Wilfork's art opening in
Freedom Springs was so memorable. It was the first time I met Rhonda
Barrett, and the first time I saw Festival of Hamburgers play.

T: That opening is referred to now in the same way as legendary.
Did it seem that way then?

L F-T: It was exciting. The Freedom Springs scene was vibrant, if
only for a small period of time. Everyone who attended the show was
happy there was something happening in their town—prior to

Hidden Wheel's inception, there was nowhere to display art, and shows were limited to bars.

T: What was it about Freedom Springs that made the art so interesting?

L F-T: I think that Freedom Springs was far enough away from established art and music scenes so that it developed in its own way, and at its own pace. The art and music from that gallery has been influential since, and that was due in part to *ArtScene's* documentation of the happenings there.

T: Certainly, Rhonda Barrett has been an outspoken advocate of the arts. Her recent contributions have been impressive. And Festival of Hamburgers' anniversary show at Knebworth was watched by millions worldwide.

L F-T: I'd be lying if I said I had any inkling of how important that evening was. I didn't. I simply thought I'd be covering a small scene, like we did in so many other cities and towns over the years. Rhonda's contributions to the art world have been a revelation. Her steadfast adherence to a set of values is unprecedented.

T: What were your first impressions of her?

L F-T: That she was brilliant. (laughter) But not for her painting. I confess that her anti-conglomerate stance seemed like a sophisticated schtick to me, one designed solely to attract the press. My impression was that she was grooming herself to be a famous painter who didn't paint. Over the years, I have come to realize, of course, that there is no schtick involved. She is deeply concerned about the human condition.

T: There were several lesser-known artists there that evening, as well. What happened to them?

L F-T: I've lost track of the members of Coxswain, except for Maddie, who played in many bands over the years. She was later in Edison's Campaign, who did very well.

The other artist that day, Max Caughin, was at the forefront of a small art movement called urban mosaicism. He became famous, then obscure just as quickly. Very little of his work still exists.

T: Why is that?

L F-T: The synthetic paint he used was pulled off the market not long after that show. It begins to disintegrate after about five years. It's tragic that his artwork no longer exists, and it's tragic what happened to him.

The band that I thought most interesting that night was Stonecipher. Bernie Reese is largely known as Rhonda Barrett's onetime lover. People forget that he was an innovative drummer. He is an experimental composer, constructing entire symphonies out of percussion. He is also a foster father. The bass player in the band, Amy Czjdeki, managed a restaurant for many years.

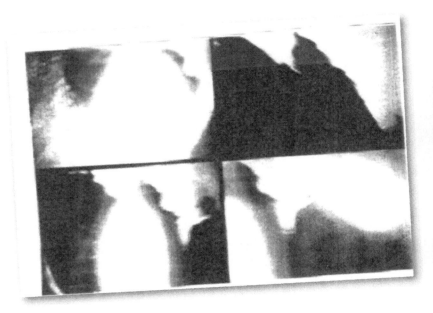

○ Chapter Four

B en called yesterday morning to ask why I hadn't gone out. I told him Amy and I went to the Dingo after we brought our gear back here. That's the problem, he said. We were all at Hub Seven. Rhonda was asking about you.

He wanted me to stop by Hidden Wheel sometime. I told him I'd be over in the afternoon, after I finished working.

I assumed he wanted some help cleaning, but the place was spotless. He was on the computer in his office.

He said he heard that we were going to be on the CD that *ArtScene* was putting out. What were we going to use for recordings?

I told him Amy was gung-ho to record in a pro studio. We didn't know where yet, though.

I've been thinking, he said. There's a lot going on here in Freedom Springs, and it seems like there might be an audience for it outside of town. He talked about the Burger and their distribution deal. It was important to have a record of everything that was happening, he said.

He had never met Seth. I told him about the Rat's Nest and the early Dead Trend shows and how much I wished I could know where everything happened. Ben nodded. We have art, and we have music, he said. Hidden Wheel is the documentation of our art scene. I am going to start a label so that we can have a record of the music, too. Stonecipher will be my first band.

I was shocked.

Still am.

I can't imagine there's much of an audience for our stuff, for one thing: people leave the room when we start playing. Two, I always

81

assumed we'd have to put everything out ourselves. And three, I never guessed that there would be someone so firmly behind us. Having Ben in our corner feels like a tremendous vote of confidence. My days proceed on a schedule. I practice rudiments and we write songs. I really enjoy myself, plus the regiment helps. I thought it would go on like this forever. Now, with money behind it, maybe we can tour and record. This feels like a good first step to see more than I ever have.

We need to find a studio. Three of the songs from the session could go to Lara Fox-Turner and the album—he said he'd work that out with Lara Fox-Turner. We'll do vinyl (vinyl!). Then we'll tour.

I can't believe any of this.

I biked over to Conforti's. I didn't know a single person working there besides Amy. She was detailing her section. I told her Ben wanted to put out our record. She screamed and hugged me.

o o o

THEY DROPPED ME OFF AT Dovestail my paintings the extra ones were in the basement another twenty-five or thirty I looked through them not my best work but still pretty good I guess better than nothing some of the colors didn't fit with the ones at Hidden Wheel so I left them at home but I could hang them someplace else maybe at Caffiend they'd let me do it I could watch people checking out my work. They wouldn't know it was me. I'd get to see their reaction to everything. If they liked it. I hope they liked it. I could go hey that's me I'm the artist they'd say hey that's great you're the guy from the exhibit I read about you then post on a messageboard when they got home about how they met the artist the guy who did that show he was going to be in the magazine what a nice guy he was I'll buy one of his paintings.

The magazine was going to come out in three months she said maybe four depended on all the bands how fast they got stuff to her she said there would be a photoshoot of me at work some of my paintings too.

○ ○ ○

JEN LAUGHED WHEN HE ASKED how Max would react. He'll buy things he doesn't need, she said. A lot of artists buy new clothes. I've already put a bee in his bonnet about that.

That's not what I'm talking about, Ben said.

It's hard for us to conceptualize, Jen said. But think about it. Most people who enter the arts take years to make a mark. Here's someone who has always fancied himself an artist, but has *never made any art*. His storyline about his alter ego—what was that name?

Faze.

That's right. It's an obvious fabrication.

How is it obvious?

Why didn't Faze's work get some kind of posthumous retrospective?

It's graffiti.

Fair enough. Why haven't there been memorial murals in his honor, then? Why has no one come forth to try and capitalize on his legacy in some way? *Because there is no legacy.* No one cares enough to disprove it is all.

How did you know all this?

I did research. It's all very ambitious—in fact, I find it quite charming. Some of the greatest artists construct their own mythologies.

It makes things easier.

I agree. In several ways. The most important being in Max himself.

I'm not following you.

After years of promoting a self which does not exist, promoting work he has for sale will come naturally to him. It will drive prices up. And he will become so smitten by the attention, and the money, that he won't question where it's coming from.

You're good.

She laughed. Do you mind if I smoke this in here?

○ ○ ○

MALE VOICE 1: This interview would have more weight if you would name yourself.[32]

MALE VOICE 2: I can't do that.

1: It's not going to look very credible. You know, anonymous guy tells a story.

2: It would look much more credible if my name was on there, but that would make my company look a lot less credible, you understand? And my wife. And my kids. I saw your ad, and I'm here. Take it or leave it.

I said, take it or leave it.

1: Okay. Anonymous is better than nothing.

2: Fine.

1: So you say that you're the one who started Rhonda Barrett out as a dominatrix.

2: That's right.

1: Can you talk about that?

2: We usually visit clients in their home cities. On the rare occasion when they come here, we pull out all the stops.
We took clients out to Christie's, one of two places we'd go with our expense account.

1: What kind of place is Christie's?

2: It's a steakhouse. Sometimes we'd go to Chez Pierre-Luc. A Michelin-starred chef from France decided to relocate to Freedom Springs, of all places.
So there were seven of us, all told. We had seven o'clock reservations, so we arrived at six and went to the bar. We got a bottle of Dom to start. It took a few minutes to arrive—they keep the bottles downstairs in the cellar.

We all wanted to get started, so we were watching the bar, waiting for that bottle. The bar server had already brought flutes to the table.

I caught a glimpse of her coming up the stairs behind the bar. I was stunned. She's a beautiful woman.

1: She is.

2: This is before she had that phase with the red hair, too. I thought she looked horrible like that. When I met her the first time, she had this natural brown hair. It was in a bun on the back of her head.

1: When did you approach her?

2: I waited until we were leaving. Everyone was hitting the can before the car service came to pick everyone up. We were pretty lit by the end. A couple nice bottles, all that steak, cappuccino. The works for our clients. And for us. (laughter)

1: She must've had men approaching her all the time.

2: Probably. Like I said, she's a beautiful woman. Even now. Have you seen pictures of her lately?

1: I have.

2: She looks great.

1: What did you say to her?

2: I introduced myself. When she didn't know my name, I told her where I worked and my office there. This is before I was (gap in tape) to give her something right away to distinguish myself from all the other men who paid so much attention to her. To establish some sort of trust.

She tried to go about her business, but she acted differently after the introduction. Even when I got to know her, it was hard sometimes to distinguish her moods, whether she was intimidated or nonplussed or furious. That's part of what made her so good. That she was so hard to read.

1: Then what?

2: I told her I had an opportunity for her. I gave her a card and told her to call.

1: And?

2: She did. Three days later, right on schedule. I asked her if she would like to make a thousand dollars an hour. She told me to go fuck myself and hung up. (laughter)

1: Wow.

2: If she had blocked her number, you wouldn't be sitting here right now, interviewing me. None of this would've happened, you understand? But she didn't. I called her back.

1: What did she say?

2: "What the fuck do you want?" (laughter)
I told her I wanted her to hear me out. And asked her if we could get a drink. She told me she wanted to see my office. Smart girl.
I scheduled her in during lunchtime. She dressed business casual, I remember. Aside from her beauty, she fit right in.
She asked me what I wanted. I told her I wanted to be humiliated.

1: What did you mean?

2: All my life I worked hard. I enjoy my life. I have a great family. I am the American dream. What they don't tell you is what happens then.

1: What?

2: The way success is portrayed is that you work all your life and overcome hardship to achieve your dream. And then the movie ends, have you noticed that?

1: The movie?

2: The movie or the book or the TV show. Happily ever after. I wasn't even fifty and had achieved everything I ever wanted. I enjoyed it all, don't get me wrong, but I thought there had to be something more.

1: How does Rhonda come into this?

2: This beautiful woman carrying cases of beer up and down a set of stairs for money. There was obviously something else about her, some hidden reservoir she could tap into if she set her mind to it. Or even if she didn't (laughter).

1: You could see all that at the restaurant?

2: I had a feeling. When you get as far as I do, you start to have feelings about people. It turns out the feeling was right. Most of mine are.

1: That's all it was? A feeling?

2: That's all it was.

1: There had to be something else.

2: That's all.

1: You didn't see anything special about her?

2: I saw what I saw.

1: So you told her—

2: I told her that I had gotten to the top, and wanted to remember what it was like to be at the bottom. I had a feeling that it would make me appreciate what I had a little more.

1: What did she say?

2: She asked questions. What sort of thing I had in mind. I told her that I wasn't after anything out of the ordinary, as far as that sort of thing goes. If she looked around online she'd get a good sense of what I was talking about.

1: Was there sex?

2: Never. It wasn't like that. I told her so up front.

1: I've read that being dominated is all about sex, and repression.

2: It wasn't like that for me. It was a kind of spiritual cleansing. It stripped away all the artifice of being so successful. People falling all over themselves to please me. It's not natural.

1: When was the first time you saw her?

2: In that capacity, the first time I saw her was a week or so later. We always met at the Wayne-Gilbreth House.

1: For how long?

2: About an hour.

1: No, how long did you meet? Weeks? Months?

2: Once every two weeks for ten years. After a certain point, it was maybe once every three weeks, once a month.

1: At a thousand dollars an hour.

2: Yes.

1: That's a lot of money.

2: Some visits were more expensive.

1: Why did your meetings become less frequent?

2: She started getting more clients. And I needed time to recover.

1: Where did she get the clients?

2: I referred a few to her. I never knew how many she had, but friends went to see her.

1: Anyone I know?

2: (laughing) You'd be shocked.

1: Try me.

2: Only one of them has died. Do you know that (gap in tape) afford it. (laughter)

1: Wow.

2: Erase that right now.

1: Hold on—

(gap in tape)

1: And you said you needed time to heal.

2: The trick for her, for me, at least, was to abuse me in ways that weren't going to be visible to my family. No marks of any kind. She got better at her craft over time.

1: What did she do?

2: There's a lot of ways a man can be led around, let's just say that.

○ ○ ○

NO ONE WAS AROUND SO I went down to the Dingo by myself had some drinks tried to tell people my art was going to be in a magazine but none of those millworkers cared one of them told me he was gonna kick my fisherman ass if I didn't shut up so I talked to some scenesters had they seen the show the other night what show they said the one with the Burger Coxswain Stonecipher that's that band with one of the people from Dead Trend they said why would I want to see a bunch of fucking Buddhist assholes trying to convert me I tried to tell them it was just the last four records but they turned around stopped talking to me so I did some shots. One! Two! Three! and went down to the river.

Pretty foggy I guess I remember walking down there I got my phone out to take some pictures all the sudden I was on the ground haha I remember saying whoops I fell then after that I don't remember anything until I woke up it was four thirty when I looked at the phone clock I was shivering the fog so I jogged home went to bed when I woke up the next day I couldn't remember how I got home at first then I saw all the photos in my phone I must've taken them before I passed out all the buildings looked huge because I was lying down. I had a different what do you call that thing perspective. I remembered Lara Fox-Turner telling me I need to reinvent myself I thought she was talking about my look I have some idea.

○ ○ ○

THE OTHER NIGHT I ASSUMED that I'd meet Rhonda over at the Dingo. I didn't get her number.

I searched for her online. Nothing. No webpage, no PalCorral. No trace. I called Ben and told him to put word out to Rhonda that I'd like to see her. He told me she didn't carry a phone. She had a landline and a pager.

○ ○ ○

ONLINE, HE FOUND:

> Dead Trend's 1995 show at Chicago's Lounge Ax was one of dubious distinctions: the band became the first (and only) act ever banned from the club, and was the last gig of bassist Denny Stairstep's tenure with the band. While onstage, (singer) Gil Falcone insisted that the reason for Michael Jordan's retirement from professional basketball was because Jordan had contracted HIV from Magic Johnson. The normally anti-sports crowd was full of basketball fans that evening, who took umbrage to Falcone's outburst. A showgoer jumped onstage and punched Falcone, resulting in a full-scale brawl that left Stairstep with two fingers broken and several members of the crowd bloody.

He then added:

> including veteran showgoer Ben Wilfork, whose nose was broken.[33]

○ ○ ○

HE WAS THERE AGAIN TODAY WHEN I WENT TO PICK UP BOK CHOY AND TOFU. HE DIDN'T SMELL AS BAD AS USUAL. HIS FULLER CHEEKS HAD COLOR. YOU, HE SAID. YOU'RE THE ONE WHO ALWAYS GIVES ME MONEY. I HAVE BEEN EATING. IT'S EASY TO EAT WITH TWENTY DOLLARS. I GAVE HIM ANOTHER TWENTY. HE LIVES ON WITH MY HELP.

o o o

I HUNG UP SOME OF my paintings at Caffiend Cordelia said no problem our PR guy's a bigshot artist now she was surprised that I charged four hundred bucks a pop but everything sold at Hidden Wheel so I might as well right? I'm lucky though because Ben asked me how to price the paintings I said twenty bucks each he was like that's too low say three I was like yeah right three bills for a CD cover who the hell would do that? I don't know who it was but on Monday he called said to come by his office he handed me a check when I got there what's this I said it's for all the work you sold how many paintings all of them he said I looked down at the check TWENTY FUCKING GRAND[34] half to me he said and a ten percent agent fee I said this is so much money! For painting! Get me some more of your work he said and I'll have it around the gallery so that people can buy it from you I had all the other paintings in the basement so I gave him those I had been painting the cameraphone shots I took the night I got drunk so those are the ones I hung at Caffiend.

I don't know why I didn't think of it before but there are all these art messageboards that people use I mean of course there are messageboards for everything so I started to see if anyone has written about my stuff no one has thing is if I start logins now it'll be so obvious that it's me pretending to be someone else timestamp registry there are these guys I know who will crack accounts for you though it's usually expensive like five hundred bucks a login but I have the corrupted files so I traded them some of those talked them down to two fifty an account for five accounts for once I can afford it the way I figure it's an investment in my work if people start buying my stuff because of posts and hype I'll make that money back quick they found some accounts no one had used for five years or more on a bunch of messageboards plus a new one just started for urban mosaicism like six months ago so I'm not such a noob over on that one.

I started setting up a webpage for myself too I have to scan my paintings when I get back to the house put up jpegs[35] of them so I can sell them online.

○ ○ ○

DONATION YESTERDAY.

Derek briefed me. They want me to come in as much as I can—three days a week is best. I have to wait two days between donations. Some weeks they'll have optional Saturday sessions. Once I go from pre-approved to approved—if my sperm is motile enough for them— I'll get eighty bucks a pop. That's close to a grand a month, if I do it right.

We read through a hygiene instruction sheet together. I initialed one of the two copies and gave it back to him when we were finished.

Derek showed me how to use the torture-looking device on the counter—put my fingers down, resting against the pins, and then punch in another passcode to confirm my identity (I'll probably get a new one for the door another one if/when I go from pre-pre-approved to pre-approved, and then from pre- to approved). After donating, I punch out on the same machine, and a label prints for the top of my specimen jar.

Derek wished me well, and went back into his office.

The fat Asian woman put her hand on the binder sitting on the counter. She asked if I wanted a video. I thought about it for a second, then said no. She gave me a look as she pushed the empty specimen jar across the counter to me. Good luck, she said. Remember to print out a label when you're finished.

Both donation room doors were locked.

I sat in the waiting area and read the reminder sheet: Wash my hands before donating. Cover the surface of the chair with paper towels. Lubrication of any kind—saliva, soap, commercial brands—was forbidden. Make donation into the jar. Do not rub member against side of jar to expunge excess donation. Remove paper towels from chair.

A guy came out of one. I didn't want to look at him, and I could tell he didn't want to look at me. I went in when he reached the end of the hallway.

I stretched my arms wide—two or three inches short of touching both walls. About the size of Ben's office.

A plastic magazine rack screwed into the wall to the left of the TV set contained copies of *Playboy* and *Hustler* and *Cheri*.[36] And above the sink was the room's sole decoration—this framed black and white photo of a woman in a bed, snarled facedown in coital sheets. A long mane of dark, wavy hair spilled over her bare back. Milky skin and drastic curves—a beautiful body. Her arms, obscured, held her ass aloft in the photo's foreground. Sheets were arranged so just a hint of ass cleavage was visible.

I laughed. I couldn't help it. Come on, big boy, the photo said. Pull out and shoot that hot load all over my back. Give it to me!

I paper toweled the chair, washed my hands, picked out a couple magazines.

Thought about it for a sec.

Washed my hands again. Dropped trou.

I am sitting bare-assed in an office chair, I thought, about to beat off into a jar and get paid for it.

The chair was still warm from the last guy's ass.

I gave my junk a little shake as I leafed through a copy of *Playboy*, looking for something good to focus on, balancing the magazine on one bare knee. The blank eye of the television stared at me. Or was someone behind it, monitoring me and my method? I shuddered. There was no way they would do that.

I found a spread of soccer girls, smiling and looking perky in stockings and baseball hats.

Okay.

I tried to focus in on one blonde girl. How we'd meet, what we'd talk about. I stopped shaking and started rubbing.

Ow.

Fuck!

I tried soap in the shower when I was little and got some down my peehole. Then, one day after school, I saw hand cream on the bathroom counter. I've been an addict ever since.

I did not want to think about being twelve. I wanted to think about the soccer girl.

I adjusted my grip, trying to hit all the sensitive spots without scuffing myself up too badly. Turned my wrist, changed my grip. Loosened.

Tightened.

Found a good spot.

The angle of my leg changed. The magazine slid to the floor.

Dammit!

Maybe the magazine could sit against the TV. That eye could stare at something else, and the whole operation would be a little easier. But the lip of shelf wasn't big enough to hold the magazine—just enough space for the set itself. I tried jamming the Playboy spine in the tiny space between wall and TV set, both sides. Neither worked.

Lost it.

The magazine wasn't working.

I turned my chair to face the photo of the woman in the poster. She'd help me.

Got it back, head craned upwards, and stared up again, trying to remember the unpainful angle of my wrist and position of my fingers for later on.

I focused in for a few minutes trying to construct the scenario which led me and the faceless woman into bed. My breath, I noticed, was becoming shorter.

The back of my neck ached. The angle of the photo.

I tried with my head facing straight forward, looking up at the curvy runway with my eyes. I couldn't focus on her back—my gaze kept landing on the list of instructions posted on the wall, below.

The TV set stared at me as I sat there with my pants puddle around my ankles.

What about the sink?

I pulled the chair over. The magazine rested comfortably on the porcelain.

When I sat, the underside of the vanity that anchored sink to wall hovered a few inches above my knees.

I took the plastic bag off the specimen jar and set it down on the left side of the vanity. Shook with my right hand and started flipping pages with my left until I found the soccer girl spread.

Re-started the reel in my head: how we met, what we'd say, how things would progress. What kind of girl she'd be. The film kept sputtering as I lost concentration and tinkered with my lube-free grip and squeeze. Dammit.

A few minutes of trial and error led to an ideal stroke. I settled in, closed my eyes, imagined dialogue and setting. Opened my eyes every few moments for some additional detail: slope of back, fingers, earlobes.

I rubbed faster.

And faster.

Ow!

A bolt of searing pain between the knuckles of my index and middle fingers. I whacked my hand on the vanity underside on the upstroke.

I touched the tips of my fingers to the palm of my hand, straightened them, repeated.

The pain subsided.

So did my erection.

Another shake, a reshift of focus.

Pushed back the chair ever so slightly.

The first bit, already scripted, replayed easily. The creation of the continuation took time—sculpting everything just so, watching, tinkering. Review took my mind off the paper towels under my bare ass and the unfamiliar footfalls outside the locked door of the jack room.

Closer now.

Closer.

The sensation of time passing in the linear sense disappeared, replaced with something like a ratchet being cranked tighter and tighter.

The early detection system went off. I was feeling so good that I almost forgot about the jar.

The jar, sitting on the vanity with the lid still screwed on tight.

I stopped.

Next time, I thought, I'll remember to take it off before I start.

I held the open jar in my hand: come on, big boy.

The ratchet loosened, then, after a few fumbling minutes, tightened.

I rubbed.

And rubbed.

Once again, the early detection system through the haze. Where I would normally close my eyes and enjoy. Except I had a purpose. And a target.

I kept at it as I stood up, pushing backwards so I wouldn't bark my knees underneath the vanity. The countertop and the magazine were both slightly higher than my knuckle as the tension continued to ratchet up tighter and tighter. Had to stand on my tippytoes to make sure I wouldn't accidentally bash my hand.

Usually I sit, but there have been times when I've stood. Tippy-toed, though, thighs doing all the support work, never.

I felt the point of no return, the five second warning.

My toes began to ache. Only a few more seconds.

I positioned the jar close to my hand, busy rubbing. It'd been a few days—the bigger, I figured, the better.

Oh, God.

My toes

Oh.

My toes

WHOAH

My left toes gave out, sending me lurching, right as I started coming.

I put my left hand down, trying to steady myself, forgetting, for a second, my objective, sending the preliminary spurt flying OVER the jar, resting completely on the counter for the briefest of moments as a consequence of my poor balance, and onto the face of the perky soccer girl I had choreographed my fantasy around.

A half-second of panic—holy shit, I fucked up *beating off*—followed by my frantic scramble to get the rest into the jar.

The secondary spurts weren't anywhere near as seismic as the first. I got the rest in. But my hopes of a new kit were already changing consistency on the page.

I wiped the face of the soccer girl with one of the paper towels from the chair. Pulled up my pants, put the remaining paper towels into the wastebasket, washed my hands, opened and closed the magazine a few times. The pages didn't stick together.

Checked the time on my cel.

Three-thirty.

I spent half an hour trying to get myself off.

When I began the punchout procedure at the desk, the lady, behind the window, gave me a look. It might've been some low-grade paranoia regarding the poor magazine girl's face, but I don't think so: *you always gonna take so long in there? We don't pay by the hour!*

Next time, I thought, I'd try a video.

○ ○ ○

HE HAD BEEN SURE TO invite reporters from the Bugle and the week-lies. Any articles that appeared online would likely serve as catalyst for print, keeping up with the blogosphere Joneses; any articles on the printed page would incite curious readers to look online at the volumes of verbiage, mostly Max's, spilled about the artists and the bands.

Those who attended could send links and say they were there. Those who hadn't would attend the next event.

○ ○ ○

IN MY THRIFT STORE VALISE ARE A TENNIS BALL, TWO PAIR OF ARMY SURPLUS HANDCUFFS AND A RIDING CROP I BOUGHT ONLINE. IN ROOM 609, HE WEARS A BATHROBE AND A PAIR OF SLIPPERS. I TELL HIM TO LIE FACEDOWN ON THE BED. I CUFF EACH HAND TO A BEDPOST. HIS PANTS ARE FOLDED IN THE WARDROBE. I REMOVE HIS WALLET AND TAKE A HUNDRED DOLLARS. OPEN, I SAY, POINTING AT HIS MOUTH. I PUT IN THE TENNIS BALL. THEN I WHIP HIS ASS ONCE AND GO DOWNSTAIRS TO THE HOTEL BAR, WHERE I HAVE A SALAD, A SANDWICH AND A FEW MARTINIS. I TAKE MY TIME AND RETURN AN HOUR AND A HALF LATER. FIFTEEN HUNDRED, I SAY. AND HE PAYS.[37]

○ ○ ○

LARA FOX-TURNER CAME TO NINE Northbrook she had those two guys with her well Maxwell she said how have you been since the show I've been doing real good I said busy hyping the magazine you are really something she said I Googled[38] you yesterday and was amazed by the number of hits I found regarding your work how many of those are your doing? I don't know I said quit the false modesty Maxwell you did most of those didn't you? I said yes. She laughed.

Where should we go she said down by the river the guy with the mock turtleneck shook his head why not I said that's where all my paintings are from too much clutter he said in this deep voice I don't think I ever heard him talk before that the fog is too hard to shoot pick someplace simpler we could go to Hidden Wheel she said no we already did Benjamin there where else I go to this coffee place every day to do my work do you know Caffiend she said very well we all got in the black Rover again I had a seat though we drove over elbow on my tacklebox between me and the turtleneck. I introduced Lara Fox-Turner to Cordelia couldn't remember what her posse were named they looked around the room said here this is it they were pointing to a brick wall where I hung my stuff none of it had sold lots of people looked at it though I always watched from my chair they were nodding most of the time. Has anyone bought anything not yet I said lots of people look how many do you have here twenty-two I said your price has gone up well you know I said I sold everything at the show so I figured did you now she said that's excellent Maxwell.

The guy with the mock turtleneck went outside the other guy started taking my stuff off the wall hey I said what are you doing you're going to stand in front of this wall the turtleneck guy said in this pretty regular voice this is the best place. Lara Fox-Turner nodded the brick wall represents the gritty urbanity that your work presents she said it's perfect the mock turtleneck guy came in with these two big lights that must've been in the trunk he started putting one together. The three or four people who were in there drinking coffee came over and started asking questions I told them I was Max Caughin formerly Mizst my paintings on the wall oops which were on the wall haha are going to be in a forthcoming article of *ArtScene* magazine this is the publisher Lara Fox-Turner he finished the first light started the other one this guy who I see in there every day doing a crossword puzzle wearing a fedora said hey. I heard about you you knew Faze. Right the turtleneck guy got one of the big lights all set up pointed at the wall Lara Fox-Turner was attaching a lens to the body of a camera that's right I said. Faze was inspirational to me when I was Mizst. I saw her look over smirk a little the guy started asking about when my work would be on exhibit as soon as we're done with the photoshoot we'll get it back on the wall I said the mock turtleneck was done taking my paintings off the wall he stacked them on the floor your work on the walls of Caffiend the guy said I had no idea the turtleneck plugged in the lights Lara Fox-Turner said are you ready Maxwell I said yes the guy said well nice meeting you and stuck his hand out so I shook it I stood in front of the wall you do realize she said that once this photoshoot happens you'll have to find a new look for yourself why I said there will be Maxwell Caughins all over the country if not the world maybe I'll start looking for the next thing now I said that sounds like a fine idea she said now stand in front of the bricks.

ο ο ο

PRACTICE YESTERDAY. AMY AND I agreed to stop writing and jamming until after the record is finished.

We played all of our songs. There are 23, if you count the early stuff. We agreed on nine right away. Amy wanted to include "Abe Lincoln, Moustache Only" on the album. I'm not crazy about it—the only song I play straight—but I told her I'd do it if we included "Chicken-shaped Patty Meal," which isn't very good but contains my favorite set of fills. She said okay. Instead of having three songs on both the album and the comp, we're giving Lara Fox-Turner "Gorilla Statue Of Liberty," "Golf Balls The Size Of Tumors" and "Buenos Noches, Minty Hands."

We got the fourteen ready, comp songs first. We decided that "Moustache" will go at the end of side one, and "Patty" will be second-to-last. The whole record will be a little longer than half an hour.

Amy said she'll find three options for studios. We'll see what we can afford. In the meantime, we're going to play the comp and album three times a practice, start to finish.

ο ο ο

HE KNEW IT WAS ONLY a matter of time before she cancelled their arrangement altogether. And he guessed she knew he knew.

She called. Are you in the office today? I have something to talk to you about.

I'll be here all day, he said.

Half an hour later, she entered, wearing a striped motorcycle jacket and jeans.

Not working today?

No clients, she said.

Then:

I came to tell you that my services will no longer be available.

He nodded his head. I couldn't endorse anyone more highly. I wish you well.

I hope you understand my need for confidentiality.

Of course, he said.

Thank you, she said. For everything. The show, especially.

Should I keep you in the loop?

For shows? Yes. I don't think I'll have anything new for another six or seven years, barring some catastrophe or revelation. But please do.

I will, he said, standing, extending his hand. She shook it, and left.

○ ○ ○

MALE VOICE 2: Has anyone else answered the ads?[39]

MALE VOICE 1: Sure. Mostly old men.

2: Thanks. (laughter)

1: Not you. The ones she played chess with.

2: Right.

1: A woman, too.

2: I didn't know about chess until the first batch of articles, ten years ago.

1: Does it, you know, surprise you?

2: The chess?

1: Yeah.

2: In some ways. She never mentioned anything to me. But on the other hand, she's so obviously smart and talented that I wouldn't be surprised to find that she could build ships in bottles, or particle accelerators.

1: So the centers.

2: Is that what this interview is about?

1: It's about filling in gaps. She never kept a journal.

2: Except for the painting.

1: That's so, you know. So small. There's more to her than that.

2: Apparently so.

1: How do you feel about them?

2: The paintings?

1: The centers.

2: There's not much that I can say about them on the record. As myself, anyway.

1: But here.

2: I am not unaware of the ironies. (laughter)

1: Is that why she did it?

2: Knowing everything I know now, I'd say no. But remember that she's a chess player. She thinks so many moves ahead.

1: You enabled her.

2: That is not lost on me. I did enable her. But the Russian. What was his name?

1: Zaitsev?

2: Yes. He also enabled her. And her teacher did. The old man. And you did. And the gallery owner.

1: But your money and your connections—

2: There are more important things.

○ ○ ○

I NEED MORE MONEY. I should have the new kit before we go into the studio.

Yesterday I put on my dress shirt and a tie and went downtown. All the temp places are within a four block radius. I made the rounds, dropping off resumes in huge office buildings. I bumped into Crank after I went to the third agency on my list. He was on his bike, wearing his spandex pants rolled up to his knees, those shoes that clip into pedals. He asked me if I had been to InTemps yet. I looked on my list—nope. He told me they hired Didier to dress up as a giant taco and pass out sample packets of some new shredded cheese.

I dropped one off there. I think I could do anything for a week if it meant having a record out.

At the other two places left on the list, too, including BrawnCorps, the place that specializes in construction. The receptionist asked me if I had experience with manual labor. I told her I was a drummer. She popped her gum.

I also applied for a credit card yesterday.

○ ○ ○

BEN'S PROPOSAL STATED THAT ALL money would be funneled directly back to the artists and musicians—the space itself, he said, would only take enough money to maintain operation. Sixty-forty was his split, always percentages, never a flat fee. The vote was unanimous.

Tax laws allowed businesses to lose money for five years. Ben considered registering Hidden Wheel Records as a hobby, but decided against it.

He discussed the money-losing aspect freely at openings and shows. Word got around, as he knew it would. They loved his stick-it-to-the-man alchemy, drugs to arts.

○ ○ ○

(Excerpted from ArtScene *magazine/pulsestream 29.6, August 2037. Used with permission.)*

ARTSCENE: Do you keep in touch with anyone from Hidden Wheel?

RHONDA BARRETT: I'm not in close touch with anyone, no. Sometimes Eli invites me to shows when they come through town. I've seen Amy a few times here and there, usually at Conforti's.

AS: Ben Wilfork?

R: I haven't seen him in years. He moved to….someplace on the East Coast. I can't remember where it was. Someplace you wouldn't think would sustain a lot of art, but that's how he does things…. Manchester, New Hampshire?

AS: He's now settled in Chicago. He says for good.

R: He's from there.

AS: How do you feel about the way he's conducted his business?

R: I think at this point everyone knows what it means when he comes to your town. Artists know what they're getting into.

AS: It's been said that he likes a certain type of art, one that is small and has a relatively consistent theme.

R: That's true.

AS: That theme seems the direct opposite of your work.

R: We're doing it for different reasons, I guess.

AS: Does it bother you?

R: Ben?

AS: Yes.

R: Like I said, artists know what they're getting into. They've seen the way Ben does things, and they know what the risks are. People know who Ben is now. He's not pretending to be something he's not anymore. So, if you want the kind of notice that Ben bestows on people, go small. Go quick.

AS: What of Bernie Reese?

R: I listen to his albums. Very interesting work. He's always been such a great drummer.

AS: The two of you were romantically linked.

R: That was a long time ago.

AS: What happened?

R: I don't have much to say about it. A conflict of interests, I guess.

AS: The painting from when the two of you were dating is unreadable.

R: And I think we both prefer to keep it that way

○ ○ ○

AMY GOT STUDIO RATES.

There's one in Duncan called Stark City. Pox Bomb did all of their Nineties records there. I downloaded a few—the drums and bass sound good. Vocals are a little high in the mix, but I think we can correct that.

There's another, in Churchill, called Big Mattress. The producer has mostly worked on metal records. The bass and drum mixes sound good, though. It's twenty-five dollars an hour cheaper to record there, but it's an hour each way. Everybody Now did a few records there before they started driving to Chicago.

I think we'll be in and out in under a week. Amy's going to call Stark City to reserve us some time.

Neither of us has any money right now. We'll put everything on the credit card.

○ ○ ○

DID YOU KNOW, BENJAMIN, THAT he's hung more paintings?

Where?

At the coffeehouse.

I believe he mentioned it to me.

He's raised his price.

He did sell out the gallery.

I have buyers lined up. He may sell more when the magazine comes out.

He's been working on paintings from a lower perspective.

When is your next show?

I haven't seen anything yet. Stonecipher is readying their album. Maybe for them.

○ ○ ○

I HAVE A JOB.

I went back to the Madison Building downtown for my interview. It's one of those places that's twenty stories high and only has three elevator buttons.

The receptionist took me to this giant mahogany lobby full of magazines about the internet. I leafed through a few before this guy came to get me for my interview. He was younger than me, wearing a suit, tassled loafers, and a ton of hair product. His teeth were so white. He introduced himself to me as Richard Johnson and took me into a room with two chairs, a window, and a giant mahogany desk.

My resume was on his desk. He asked what I did before I became a freelance copywriter. I told him about the bookstore job, omitting my time at Conforti's. (I didn't mention the band, either—it seemed safer not to.) He asked if I considered myself a creative person. I said I did.

He asked if I had heard of dramatic persuasion. I said no.

Here's where he really got going. Let me try and remember what he said:

"Studies have shown that attention spans have been decreasing drastically in the last ten years. Some theorists place responsibility for this phenomenon squarely on the shoulders of the internet."

Makes sense, I said.

"In the past, the average advertisement on television lasted for thirty seconds. Typically, viewers stopped responding after about twenty seconds."

I said sure.

"Nowadays, though, with the advent of pop-up advertising, the average American's psyche is programmed in such a way as to try and filter out invasive advertising. As a result, new information typically engages a viewer for an average of *eight seconds*."

Eight seconds?

"*Eight seconds*," Richard Johnson said, grinning. "So advertisers are trying to do everything they can to reach audiences for longer than eight seconds. Studies show that every engaged second after the eighth increases the chances of a consumer purchasing a product by *three percent*."

I told him it sounded interesting. What were the specifics?

"The New Environment Coalition is a great supporter of dramatic persuasion," he said. "In their current campaign, they are conveying their specific interest in preserving South American rainforests[40] from further destruction."

I told him rainforests were important.

"Have you ever had a Tropical Nut Munch?"

No, I said.

"Tropical Nut Munch," he said, leaning back into his chair, "is typically sold in the granola and power bar market. But the NEC doesn't think that it quite fits into either demographic smoothly. For one thing, it is neither a granola bar nor power bar per se. Each bar consists mostly of nuts harvested by tribal farmers in the rainforest. And a percentage of profit from each bar gets contributed directly back into NEC's rainforest preservation fund. A consumer can feel confident that he or she is contributing something to society by purchasing the product."

Great.

"I should mention, in the interest of full disclosure, that occasionally domestic nuts augment the bars. The tribes that we work with are all fantastic people—have you ever been to the rainforest?"

No.

"I don't get out of the office too much," he said, looking around the room, "but when the NEC offered me a chance to go, I was overjoyed. I am always happy to help out our clients here at InTemps. What I saw was just remarkable. The tribe are some of the kindest people you'll ever meet. There I was, a complete stranger in a mosquito net, and I was handed nuts that were *just picked*. You'll never taste a finer nut than one that is freshly harvested."

I told him I was interested in the product.

"But because the natives lack the sophisticated factories that we have here in the United States, those nuts, tasty though they may be, do not always have the . . . bite necessary to make Tropical Nut Munch the best experience possible. Their nuts do not always have the right amount of crunch. We have tried to amend this problem by referring to them as 'munch' instead of 'crunch'—'munch' is much more tactile—but sometimes domestic nuts must be introduced."

I told him I understood.

"Very good. So," he said, "might you be interested in dramatically persuading customers to save the rainforest by purchasing Tropical Nut Munches?"

Yes, I said.

"Excellent! When can you start?"

As soon as possible, I said.

"We typically schedule four hour days. You do have a valid driver's license?"

I nodded.

"There is no lunchbreak, but you can feel free to incorporate eating and drinking into your dramatic persuasions. We will provide bottled water and Tropical Nut Munches for you."

Great.

"Tropical Nut Munches provide a full complement of vitamins and nutrients. Two bars provide everything you need *for an entire day!*" He smiled. "But we think you'll eat more than just two."

Maybe I will.

"As we discussed before, every second beyond the eighth increases the chance of purchase by three percent. To that end, we will be asking you to stage a series of dramatic interpretive actions in a constructed environment."

I asked him what he meant by dramatic interpretive actions.

He slid a manilla folder across his leather desk blotter, smiling. "Please. Take a look."

I opened the folder. Several glossy photographs were inside, each depicting what looked to be a clear glass moving van filled with plants.

"As you can see," Johnson said, "the New Environment Coalition's Portable Environment Simulation is self-contained and looks very authentic. We have simulated the rainforest environment using the newest polymers and chemical blends. There is not a more authentic looking rainforest-like environment simulation anywhere in the country," he said. "And the van itself is a hybrid! Environmentally conscious *and* it gets great gas milage!"

I didn't know what to say.

"You will have a variety of outfits to choose from," he said. "Studies show that repeat viewers will find several different choices best. We will provide outfits suitable for safari, tourism, and harvest."

Harvest?

"You are, of course, Caucasian," he said. "The use of any darkening agents is strongly discouraged. There are several lighter-skinned tribesman in the rainforest. And any dissonance that a viewer might feel about your skin color is a bonus. If a consumer wonders about the authenticity of the presentation, he or she will likely research the rainforest independently. Time spent researching virtually assures that that potential consumer will purchase one of our products."

Smart, I said.

"For that reason, the harvest option is most favorable. Do you have any visible tattoos or piercings?"

No, I said.

"Good. That will increase the believability of the presentations."

I asked where dramatic persuasions take place.

"We have a list of suggested locales," he said. "At your orientation, the managing dramatist will show you the preferred areas. Studies have shown that repeated instances of dramatic persuasion in one area begin to lose their potency, so you will be alternating cites for the three-week duration of your employ. Areas with high concentrations of pedestrian traffic are best."

Three weeks in the back of a glass truck. Selling granola bars. But we need money to record. If nothing else, maybe I'll get some material out of it. I'll try and think up new beats in my head, or write lyrics about it or something.

I asked how much money I'd be making.

"You will be compensated quite handsomely for your time," he said, "with the chance to become a managing dramatist yourself. If everything goes well, and we trust that it will, you will have the chance to oversee similar campaigns for this and other products."

Hourly, or salary?

"Of course." He reached into his desk and produced a sheet of paper. He wrote something, folded the sheet, and pushed it across the table to me. "This is the hourly rate we offer."

Twenty dollars an hour.

"Because you are a creative self-starter," he said, "we think you're perfect for the job."

I told myself it won't be that bad. At least I didn't have to dress as a taco.

"Do we have a deal?"

I nodded.

"Excellent!"

It's two weeks. I start Monday. That's eight hundred dollars, before taxes. Half of a drumkit, or three days in the studio.

○ ○ ○

(Excerpted from ArtScene *magazine/pulsestream 29.6, August 2037. Used with permission.)*

ARTSCENE: Can you discuss your artistic process?

RHONDA BARRETT: In what way?

AS: How you conducted your day-to-day work.

RB: My first canvas was a happy accident. I bought one big piece, thinking I might cut it. But I liked the large size, so I began.

I've had the loft space for years. I've always had my canvases on the floor while I work. After a point I can fold them to take up less space, if I need to. But I like being able to see everything I've done. I can walk or even crawl across the blank canvas if it's on the floor.

AS: When do you work?

RB: Initially I painted before I went to bed. This was for the first year or so. I began to realize, over time, that some of what I was painting each night wasn't as important to me the next day when I'd wake up. If you look at my earliest entries they're very stream-of-consciousness.

There's nothing wrong with that early work, but as I continued painting I realized that my recollections should be more focused. Ebbs and flows would emerge through a more well-thought out approach. To that end, I began writing my work before I painted it.

AS: Do you consider yourself a writer?

RB: I do. I'm the author of one very long real-life memoir. Maybe a little too long for some readers. (laughs) But because it's on canvas, critics think I'm a painter.

Once I felt comfortable, I imposed a word count on myself. I tried for sixty a day. Seventy was fine.

AS: Why sixty?

RB: Why not? (laughs) I liked the way the number felt, I suppose. And there are sixty seconds in a minute, obviously. And sixty minutes in an hour. I thought the number would help reflect the passage of time, and would keep the number of canvases manageable.

AS: What do you mean by that, manageable?

RB: If my life's work was thirty canvases, there would be less impact on a viewer than if there were seven, say. Seven means you can see them all at the same time. It shows my mortality in a more tangible way.

AS: There are some entries that have been longer than sixty words. Or seventy.

RB: Yes. Sometimes going over can't be avoided.

AS: Does the way critics respond to your work bother you?

RB: I stopped paying attention.

AS: Why is that?

RB: The first bit of recognition I got was after the Hidden Wheel opening. In fact, it was in *ArtScene,* back when it was only a magazine. Imagine that! (laughs)

AS: The piece was flattering.

RB: It was. But it wasn't entirely accurate.

AS: How so?

RB: My no camera policy was used as a story angle. I said I wanted the work to speak for itself, which was certainly true.
Anyone who spent any time with my work would've seen that I was discussing topics which were potentially very controversial. My day job was there for all to see. I didn't say that photos would allow me to be identified easily—I thought it was obvious, from my work, why I didn't want images of me to be reproduced.
The no camera policy became something it was not very quickly. And it bothered me. So I stopped paying attention.

AS: Anyone could have taken photos of you at an opening.

RB: I stopped attending them after a point, so the work *did* speak for itself.

AS: But at that first one, anyone could have taken pictures of you.

RB: I was young, so I hadn't thought everything out as well as I should've. No harm was done by those early gallery shows, or when I completed canvases.

AS: But you're doing this interview, so your work isn't speaking for itself.

RB: Touche. (laughter) At this point, I prefer to think of this interview as a commercial for my Centers rather than for my work, though my work continues. Plus, I'm not getting any younger.

AS: Over the years you have been portrayed as something of a hermit.

RB: That's news to me.

AS: You weren't aware that you've been portrayed as an eccentric?

RB: I *am* an eccentric. (laughter) Not just in my work, either—in my life choices. I've never been married, have only had one significant relationship. I continue to keep odd waking hours. I worked as a dominatrix, and delivered bread to restaurants on a bicycle. It's all in my work. It sounds as if the portrayals are accurate.

But as far as being a hermit goes, it's simply not true. I keep to myself, but I know the people around me.

AS: What do you think they think about you?

RB: Probably "there's that weird lady." (laughs)

AS: Were you ever worried that your photo would be taken when centers opened?

RB: I chose not to attend the initial few grand openings. Too fancy for me. But once I retired from the business I worried less. Everyone who worked and volunteered at the centers was immensely respectful of my privacy.

AS: There have been a few leaked photos.

RB: Before my retirement?[41]

AS: Since, I think.

RB: No harm done, then.

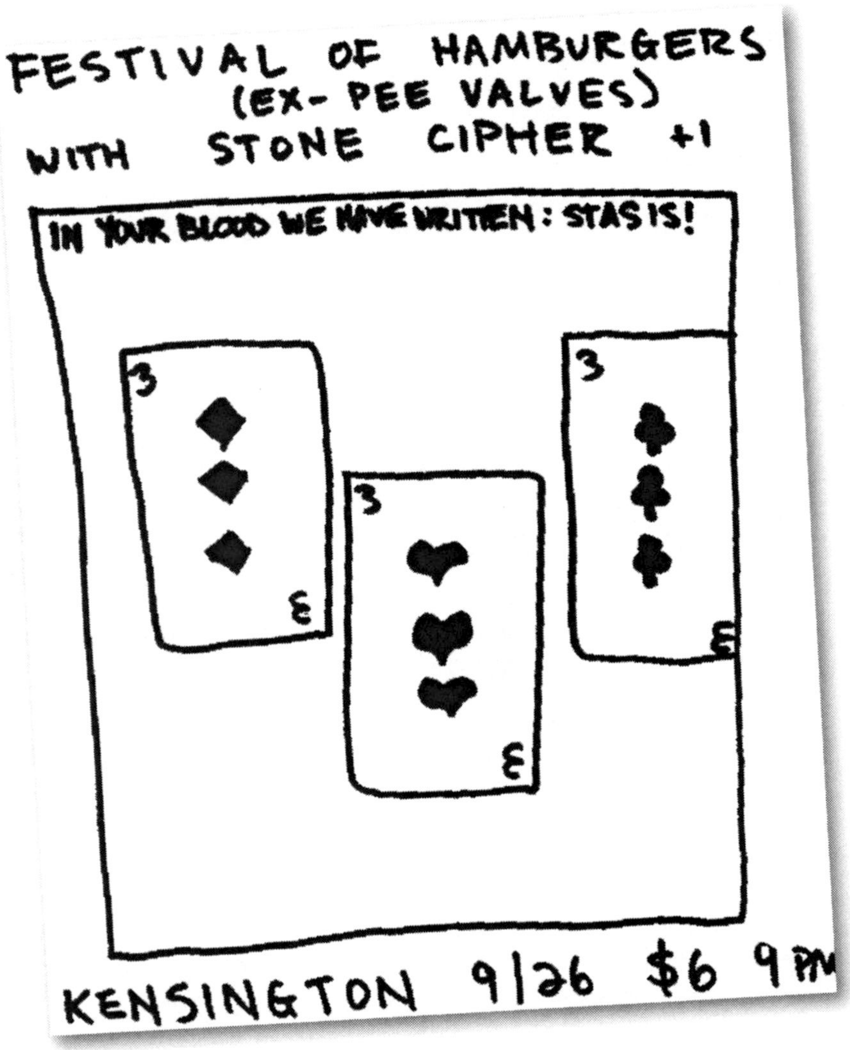
FESTIVAL OF HAMBURGERS
(EX- PEE VALVES)
WITH STONE CIPHER +1
IN YOUR BLOOD WE HAVE WRITTEN: STASIS!
3
3
3
KENSINGTON 9/26 $6 9 PM

◯ Chapter Five

W e decided to go with Stark City.[42] They have off-time rates after nine pm. Amy talked to an engineer (who is a big Dead Trend fan) and told him about our stuff. He said that if we play live, we should be able to bang everything out fine. We're going to have two-hour practices every day until we start, a week from Monday, and play the record four times through at each practice. The only problem is sleep. For three days I'm going to be dramatically persuading starting at ten-thirty, probably getting home at six. Four hours, tops. Hopefully it won't be too bad.

I called Amy and asked if I could borrow her car. I told her I'd drive her to work. She said okay. I took her down to Conforti's, then went over to Music Sheik and put the new kit on my credit card.

I spent the entire afternoon playing. I'm a little behind on my clients. The thing is that I don't really mind. I'm still amazed by the long sustain all of the toms have. The second crash is great—I don't have to use the ride as a crash any more.

I called Rhonda today. No answer.

◯ ◯ ◯

DEAR NEW HIRE,

The New Environment Coalition, in conjunction with InTemps, welcomes you to our team of skilled dramatic persuasionists.

Your job, as a dramatic persuasionist, is to fully develop a character who will form an emotional tie with viewers. Connecting with one viewer every fifteen seconds may seem like a daunting task at first, but with some practice, your dramatic persuasions will entice viewers to purchase Tropical Nut Munch bars and save the rainforest.

Possible scenarios:

Tourist

A tourist on a group expedition becomes separated from his or her tour group. S/he is in a panic. The tourist discovers a cache of Tropical Nut Munch bars, which makes him/her feel secure that help is on the way.

Safari

A safarigoer is chased by an invisible predator. The safarigoer produces a Tropical Nut Munch bar to ward off the predator. The predator adapts a more kindly attitude towards the safarigoer after being fed a Tropical Nut Munch bar.

Harvest

1. *A native harvests nuts from a tree. The native is proud to be harvesting nuts to provide a positive contribution to the environment.*
2. *A native harvests nuts from a tree. The native is proud to be harvesting nuts to provide a positive contribution to the local economy.*
3. *A native enjoys a tasty Tropical Nut Munch bar.*

o o o

I PAGED RHONDA THIS MORNING, around ten.

She called back around one. Her voice was lower than I'd remembered it.

Hello, I said, I'm looking for Rhonda.

She said Who is this?

Bernie. Uh, Bernie Reese. From the opening. Stonecipher.

Who gave you this number? Her voice changed—it wasn't so deep anymore.

Ben did, I said.

Did she say "sonofabitch?" I think she did.

She told me I called her work line. There was a landline in her loft, with an answering machine, if I wanted to call her in the future.

I asked if I could see her. She goes to bed in the afternoon and sleeps until early evening because of her bread delivery job. She asked if I wanted to get some breakfast with her around nine-thirty at night sometime this week. I told her okay. We're going to meet at City Diner, downtown, a week from Thursday.

○ ○ ○

FORTY-EIGHT HOURS BETWEEN DONATIONS. THERE'S an optional Saturday this week. Then next week will be Tuesday and Thursday.

○ ○ ○

I WENT TO ORIENTATION TODAY in a warehouse not far from Hidden Wheel. I say orientation, but it was a bored security guard who took me to a room with a DVD player.

In the video, a smiling man at a desk said how happy he was that I joined the team. He showed me how to use the climate controls in the Portable Environment Simulator, and how to get into and out of the costumes. One of the dashboard levers is a tone generator, which plays what he called a scenario reminder. Different markets have different attention spans, he said, and the setting will vary from city to city. The most common setting is fifteen seconds, which I'll be using.

Then there was a big speech about dramatic persuasion. The camera zoomed in to show how serious the narrator was. Apparently there's a videocamera in the back which monitors performance standards—the man didn't say who was doing the monitoring.

The guard took me to a garage to show me the PES. It's about the size of a U-Haul truck, all clear. One side has the Tropical Nut Munch logo in two foot-high letters across the bottom of the plexi, at about the level of the 'earth.' He said that we should go for a test drive.

A curtain of clear plastic strips separated the cab from the rainforest. The guard (who introduced himself as Jim once we got in) told me to turn on the climate control, high setting. A little warm air blew through the strip curtain.

There's no place to change except for the cab, he said. I'll have to get into costume at the warehouse, then drive to the sites. He told me to make sure I had my license with me. Any cop who pulled me over wouldn't understand a native driving a glass track full of fake plastic trees.

We got on the highway. It handled fine. Then downtown. The narrow streets weren't as bad as I thought.

After we got back to the garage, the guard told me the last thing was to get into the back to see how it felt. I killed the ignition. Keep it on, he said, the back gets hot quick. I started it back up. I almost forgot to tell you, he said, lowering the passenger side sunvisor, there's a gas card up here. Nothing but gas. No snacks or magazines or anything, okay? You need to fill it up every day. The tank is on your side, in the back. If you run out, the fans won't work.

I pushed through the plastic strips into the rainforest and started sweating almost immediately. Jets of cooling air blew through floor vents and shook the tropical plants and tree branches.

Jim yelled that he was going to start the tone generator as I paced. Two big steps across the back, and three up and down.

The tone sounds like a hospital hallway—always there, even though I couldn't figure out where it was coming from.

I start Monday.

ooo

Job, Day 1. God. Just horrible. Twenty bucks, but still. A grass skirt? Facepaint? I'm an idiot.

The tone is the worst. I didn't think it would be. At first, it wasn't bad. After an hour, I could feel it. My body knew it was coming. I felt the beeps in my spine. Over and over. Strangest thing.

I'm wearing earplugs today. I hope it helps.

I don't want to go. I did the math: two hundred forty beeps an hour. Nine hundred sixty scenarios per day. I might count them tomorrow. Maybe that would help.

People outside staring. I tried to avoid eye contact. Some little kid tapping the glass. Thank God I didn't see anyone I know.

I wish I didn't need the money.

Job, Day 3. It's easier with a hangover. Amy and Seth and I went out to the Dingo Tuesday night. I had four beers. Getting up yesterday morning was hard. But my head hurt, so I concentrated on the pain instead of the beep. It's not so bad with earplugs.

Instead of restarting my ways of thinking every fifteen seconds, I tried to keep four storylines going in my head today:

- The safarigoer is the survivor of a plane crash, looking for some sign of civilization,
- The safarigoer is hot on the trail of a hidden village which contains the Fountain of Youth,

- The safarigoer is searching for his ancestry, which in some way ties into a fabled village, and
- The safarigoer is walking around in the jungle looking for villages near harvestable nut trees.

It was hard keeping all four stories going in my head, but after an hour or so I got it. I thought of each story as a limb, doing something different.

Kids tapping on the glass again today.

I'm going to rotate the personas to keep things fresh. Today is native again. It's my least favorite, but I bought some Venerable at the corner store after work and drank three of them. I have a low-grade headache today, no water or ibuprofen before I went to bed.

I'm going to make a donation today after I get done, just in case. My date with Rhonda is tonight.

JOB, DAY 4. We were at the diner from nine-thirty until one, when Rhonda said she had to get to the bakery. I bought a plate of fries neither of us wanted after we finished our breakfasts so we could keep sitting there. I was starting to get tired, even though I drank coffee the whole time. I thought not getting any sleep would be as good, or better, as a hangover for the truck today. We'll see. Got about four hours.

Rhonda. Wow. She played chess for ten years when she was growing up, in leagues and against the old men in front of Le Petit Chapeau. She says she can see the way the game is going to unfold. Each piece has a series of possibilities attached to it, which change depending on how the other person moves *their* pieces. She was laughing at herself when she talked about it. I asked her if we could play a game sometime. She says she hasn't played since Zaitsev, the smartest player ever, was beat by a computer named Bigger Pink. I got her to agree to play me.

She says she started worrying about computers because of Zaitsev. If a computer can play chess, the most elegant game (she said that: *the most elegant game*), what else are computers going to be able to do? Are they going to write books? Make music? Take over the world? She thought all this before scientists named it the Singularity, when computers make humans obsolete. I asked her if there was going to be a big humans-vs.-computers war. She smiled and said no.

But because computers are computers, she doesn't think they're ever going to be able to have days. There will be mechanical failure, but computers will always back themselves up. Days are meaningless to them because when the Singularity happens, they'll live forever.

The thing we have that they don't is a sense of mortality.

That's why she paints. Four, maybe five canvases, she says, before she's done. She'll never sell her work. She'll tour it, though. She says that her dream is to figure out some way to help people directly. But she hasn't figured out exactly how she's going to help people yet.

I told her about our tour. She asked how long I've been playing drums. She asked me when we met, she said, but I didn't get a chance to answer her. I told her about two years,[43] since Dad died.

When I used to stand in the corner, facing the wall, singing "America the Beautiful," I wanted to kill him. But I knew I couldn't. It would be letting him win. So I pushed it as far down as I could. I thought it'd go away when he died. I sat with him every day and waited. It didn't.

It helps not being around people all the time—in retrospect, I can't believe I was stupid enough to even try working at a restaurant. It was the money, I guess. I was always aware of it. I got used to it.

The drums don't make any of that disappear They just make it different, like a well pulling oil from the ground. I told Rhonda that and she knew what I was talking about right away. All those years of being anchored made it grow. I can't ever make up for it, but I can see all the things I never got a chance to while Dad was sick. I schedule and work hard.

She asked if my father was the reason why I didn't play music on the beat. I told her I thought the drums sounded better like that.

Her mom died when she was a teenager, she told me. Things had been rocky between her parents before that, which she thinks might be part of the reason she played chess so much. Because it got him out of the house. Without him, she said, she wouldn't have her life's work, but she wonders what it might be like not to have life's work. To just be.

We're going to see each other again sometime this week.

JOB, DAY 5. Got up at noon today. Noon! I can't remember the last time I slept that late.

Persuaded as a native yesterday after my date. A bunch of kids in all black came by and mouthed the word 'racist' at me during the lunch rush. It was hard to keep persuading.

We ran through the sets again last night. I kept fucking up. We played through. Amy was pissed. I'm worried about getting enough sleep for recording next week.

I'm going to make a donation today, then go to practice.

JOB, DAY 6–8. Hard to remember which day is which. I haven't been here since Sunday morning.

Kids threw tomatoes at the glass yesterday. Signs this time: "RACIST," "BOYCOTT COLONIALISM." I looked up Tropical Nut Munch earlier this morning (I'm not sure why I didn't look it up earlier) and found some articles about their environmental practices. Richard Johnson kept telling me about how the company empowered the locals by providing them with employment. What he forgot to mention was that they only hire *light-skinned* locals. And the tribes that live in the harvest areas get displaced. There's an article online about a guy who was shot with a tranquilizer dart because he wouldn't leave his tribe's ceremonial gravesite. The TNM people were afraid he'd hack them to death with his machete. This has come out in the past few weeks. No way I'm wearing that native costume for my last two days.

I called Rhonda again on Sunday (her landline this time) and left a message. She told me that I could come over after work and take a nap if I wanted—she slept until nine, usually, but didn't mind getting up a little early to get some dinner before I went to the studio.

She has a loft space not so far from Hidden Wheel and the PES warehouse, in what used to be a bearing factory. A creaky freight elevator took me up to the fourth floor.

Everything about the place seemed a little too perfect, like the elevator: I pushed her huge metal door open and saw dust floating through cartoon sunlight spilling through windows facing the sun. A little stool with an overfull ashtray and a spaghetti sauce jar full of paintbrushes sat on the unused part of the canvas on the floor.

She told me sometime over the last few days, I can't remember exactly when, that the blank part stayed on the floor, and the finished stuff got pulled onto the wall. The amount of wallspace taken up was a sign of progress, she said, and the everyday comings and goings over the unused portion added a dimension to her work. (She said I didn't have to take my shoes off, but I did anyway. Too weird not to.)

There's a kitchen/dining room area in the back left, and her room on the back right. She was sleeping in this huge bed when I got there the first day. She didn't wake up when I got in. She just pulled me close.

We slept for a while. And we made out for the first time. She hadn't brushed her teeth, but I didn't mind.

She asked me about the studio over coffee. Was I nervous? Had I been before? I told her about fucking everything up at practice because I've been drinking too much to make dramatic persuasion easier. She said I could come over and take naps afterwards, if that would help. I told her it would. (And I'll be taking naps today and tomorrow. I'm not sure about next week yet. I'm worried about making donations. I didn't think I'd be seeing someone while I donated. I need the money, though.)

She hasn't painted for a while. What she liked to do was get up and think about what happened the day before. She said it's the things that you remember first when you wake up that are the most important. She sits at the kitchen table and writes everything down—this is by hand—and then re-writes it all so it's short. She tries for sixty words or less. There are important days, like her first day of work, which take up more space (more about that in a second). Then, based on how she was feeling that day, she uses a paint color to match her mood and paints out her day in these tiny, intricate letters. I took a look at them while she was sleeping yesterday when I got back from the studio: they're so similar that they look computer-generated, like a font. She's so exact and so precise. She wants the same number of lines per week in all of her work so that the passage of time is visible in a specific way. But since she finished her first one, she says she's been having trouble. She's not sure how, but somehow she got off track. She keeps writing every morning, but hasn't been painting much. Once a week at most—I haven't seen her work on the canvas at all. She says she's worried about how the gaps will look.

I asked her how she could afford such a nice place by delivering bread at night. She was an artist, but her coffee was French press and the loft has so much sun that realtors could talk about 'natural light' and make a killing off the place.

She made me sit down (this is the second day of napping). Before she started delivering bread she worked at some fancy restaurant downtown as a bartender. One of her customers is some bigshot CEO—she wouldn't tell me who it was—who liked her dreads and offered her a job beating him up.

She whips their asses, and sometimes they're naked, but that's it. Which I've never heard of before. But the way she explained it to me is that the CEO was so used to people saying yes to him that he needed someone who would say no, no matter what. And that includes sex. He always asks her, she says, but she's never going to. If she did (which she says she doesn't want to do anyway) she wouldn't get paid any more. She's using the power this guy gives her to live in a loft and paint.

When she finished, she sat there, looking at me. I could see her eyes going back and forth, from me to the door.

I thought about how stupid I felt running around in the back of a glass truck, wearing a grass skirt.

I asked her if it made her feel better, hitting those guys. Or whatever it was she did. She told me it did, and that the money would help her help others. She just didn't know how yet.

I told her about going to the hospital, to see Dad. I kept waiting for him to say something. To realize. To make reference to it. Like son, I'm sorry I've been such a bastard or you turned out okay or thanks for coming to see me every day even though I used to keep you in the dark. And about how I could do anything I wanted when he died. I had to do something. I had to figure something out.

No one knew about that before I told her.

She works, bikes around, and paints. She has a regiment.

I went back yesterday. We had diner food the first night, and Thai food on Tuesday. Wednesday she made me a big dinner of tofu and bok choy and rice noodles. She's a good cook.

I worried things would be weird yesterday, because of her telling me about her job, and me telling her about Dad. But they weren't. I think maybe I wanted them to be.

We ate and I talked about the record and learning to play. She asked me if I went into a trance. I told her it was more like living in a world where there was only one thing. I feel strong when I'm playing, like my body saves energy for drums in a hidden tank. She says she feels the same when she's working.

Her place feels like a vacation. I like it, but I'm not sure how I'm going to get back on schedule. I'll have to bust my ass today and tomorrow to finish the catalogues.

I haven't really written about recording yet, either. Every day, Amy and Seth picked me up at the PES warehouse and we drove down to Stark City. It's a nice place. I've never been to a studio before, so I didn't know what to expect. A lot of bands fly in to record with this guy Gil,[44] who did post-hardcore stuff in the nineties. There's dorm rooms there for out-of-towners, plus a pool table, some video games, movies, a TV set, a kitchen, books, magazines, and a huge coffeemaker. Seth came all three nights and sat in the control room, reading old *Rolling Stone* magazines and smoking.

We didn't record with Gil (too expensive). We were with Kush, one of his other engineers. The name's not short for anything—he's just Kush.

On the first day, I got frustrated because I didn't realize it was going to take so long to set up. He had to figure out the best way to mic the drums to get the live sound we wanted. One in the kick, one for each tom, the snare, some mics on stands ('room mics'), and some overheads which got both me and Amy. I had to sit there and hit, play each one, the whole kit. I felt like we were wasting the first night.

Once everything was set up, we blasted right through it. The naps helped me out, I guess. Most of our songs were first takes—maybe two of them took multiple tries. Some of them weren't perfect, like when I blew the roll on "Freshmen and Winos." My mistake sounded cool, so we kept it and moved on.

I can't believe how easy the process was. Kush said that we did it the right way. Most bands don't practice as much as we do before they come in, he said, especially on their first records. "Too many goddamn Fleetwood Mac wannabes" is what he said.

Amy did all the vocals yesterday. Kush thought we should do shoutalong backing vocals on a few of the songs, so he and Seth and I all got in a room and yelled into a microphone for the chorus of "The Esperanto of Jetlag."

We have a rough mix done. I played it for Rhonda. She loves it. It'll sound better once we get it mastered. We sent it to a place in Boston that Kush recommended. The guy there has done all these metal and punk records, so we'll be a good fit.

I don't want to go to work today. Again. Two days will be fine. Eight hours. I'll try to make a donation before my last shift tomorrow. I'll be ready by then.

JOB, DAY 9. I did tourist yesterday. Two hours in, I heard thumps against the glass. Tomatoes. Out the corner of my eye, I saw the kids wearing all black, in skimasks. Their signs said: BOYCOTT COLONIALISM, RACIST, INDIGENOUS ARE PEOPLE TO.[45] I walked around the PES, trying to keep all four limbs going. It was hard not to be distracted. I stopped when I saw it wasn't just three kids out there. It was closer to thirty.

More tomatoes came flying at the sidewalk side glass. I couldn't see through the red haze. But I could see the glass spiderwebbing when their rocks hit.

The only way out was through the cab. I thought if I tried to run, they'd probably beat the shit out of me. I had to stay inside.

There wasn't anything to defend myself with. Nothing.

They surrounded the PES. Then a crowd gathered to watch. I thought about driving away, but I would've killed someone.

I stood in the middle of the truck, in a patch of fake trees, waiting.

Impact ran up my legs each time a rock struck the glass. I had never noticed how thick it was. I imagined it caving in. Would they stone me to death? Would they drag me out?

The rocks stopped. The glass held.

The PES began to tilt back and forth.

Through the clear side, I saw a row of skimasked heads rocking in time with the sway. A few of them walking around, with their signs, videocameras. But most of them were trying to tip it.

Each sway became a lurch. I felt my stomach in my throat.

I lost my footing and fell against the spiderwebbed red glass.

I had to get out.

I grabbed a fake tree and righted myself, then lunged through the plastic strips into the cab. I barked my shin against the gearshift as I scrambled over the driver's side seat and out, headfirst, onto the sidewalk.

The crowd yelled for me. I couldn't tell what they were saying when I landed. But it was for me. I knew that.

Hands under my armpits, dragging me away. A skimask poked a videocamera into my face and called me a pig.

It was a man wearing all blue workwear the way Max used to. A few people were with him. Their faces were wide and open. My back slammed against a wall, hard.

Are you okay?

I held up my right arm (the good one). It was scraped raw. I moved it a few times. I think so.

My head was clearing.

What were you doing in there?

Dramatically persuading, I said.

Wadsworth Vending, one patch read. Hal, read the other.

The crowd started to yell.

Jesus, Hal said. Look at that.

The PES stood at an angle for a second and righted itself.

Over the crowd: PUSH!

It teetered and went over. The glass held, somehow. A huge thud echoed with impact. The trees and shrubs inside listed towards the sidewalk

It's a good thing you got out of there, Hal said. You could've been hurt.

Cheers from the skimasks. They threw their signs to the sky. One of them ran over with the videocamera. I don't know if it was the same guy as before.

What do you think of that, you capitalist pig?

Leave this man alone, Hal said, sticking his hand in the camera. He ain't hurt nobody.

○ ○ ○

The police called this morning to ask a few follow-up questions.

I called Richard Johnson yesterday when I got home from the police station. He apologized and promised that I'd get paid for the lost day. He said I should call if I ever need more work.

Max called yesterday afternoon. He asked how it felt to be famous. I told him I didn't understand.

He told me to look at Scoopdumpster.

The video the skimasks shot was up. They called themselves the Indigenous Land Liberation Front. Scenes shot over the course of a few days. Me, dressed as a native, walking around in the PES. They called me a gerbil on a wheel and threw tomatoes. The guy with the camera in my face. I looked horrible, pale and beaten.

After the flip, the video cut to a skimasked guy sitting in a wicker chair holding a spear. Unless hiring practices were changed in the rainforest, he said, more trucks would be flipped.

Amy knocked on my door when she got back from work. She said she was surprised I was home. I told her I needed some time to myself. I'd been sleeping, mostly.

She asked if I knew that I was all over the internet. I told her Max had called to tell me.

This is only going to help us, she said.

What do you mean?

When we go on tour. It's good promotion.

I got my ass kicked in that video, I said.

People will know it.

They might, I said. But they'll know me as the guy wearing a grass skirt.

It'll help, she said. We have to use it.

I'm not so sure. People online are already rooting for those guys in the skimasks. What were they called again?

You watch, she said. It'll help.

AHOY:

Whaleship at sea

COXSWAIN
FESTIVAL OF HAMBURGERS
STONECIPHER (X-DEAD TREND)
9 PM FRIDAY 26TH SIX $
@ KENSINGTON 122 RIVER ST.

◯ Chapter Six

(Excerpted from ArtScene *magazine/pulsestream 29.6, August 2037. Used with permission.)*

ARTSCENE: You have refused, on many occasions, to talk about your time with Bernard Reese.

RHONDA BARRETT: That's right.

AS: Why is that?

RB: I have been remarkably open about my life. It's all on canvas for everyone to see, save for one period of less than a year. Think about it—my whole life, starting in my early twenties.

On the few occasions I've granted interviews, I've been asked questions about my work in the industry. I have no problem answering them. Interviewers have understood, and respected, boundaries in discussing my work: the recipients of my services will remain anonymous. There are lives involved beyond mine and the clients'. These men had families. Some were here on business. There's no need to name names.

Bernie and I are very similar in many ways. We connected. There was a period of time where we lived together. Some of our time together was very good. Some of it was not. One of my paintings was accidentally destroyed. These are the facts that I am comfortable disclosing. They're very much out in the open. Bernie hasn't said anything more because he doesn't feel comfortable doing so. Neither do I.

I understand that people want to know what happened. Part of that hunger for knowledge is my decision to include the unfinished canvas as part of my life work. But, at the same time, if I *didn't* include it, there would be speculation as to why there was such a gap. I feel like I can't win.

AS: By framing your answer in that way, it seems that you're alluding to some disastrous consequences.

RB: In what way?

AS: I understand—I think we all understand—that you don't want to name names of your clients. The way you've framed your answer, it seems as if there might be similar connotations to discussing your relationship.

RB: I made the comparison I did to emphasize that there are boundaries which I don't think should be crossed. The media have been respectful of my desire not to name my clients. I hope they—you, Lara—can be similarly respectful of my desire not to discuss the end of our relationship.

AS: What about the beginning? What attracted you to him?

RB: I feel comfortable saying we're very much alike. When Bigger Pink defeated Zaitsev, I felt groundless. I didn't know why to go on, or how. I drifted, until my work found me. I think Bernie felt like that for a long time, adrift, until his father passed away. He pursued his drumming as hard as he could afterwards.

AS: Have you listened to his recent compositions?

RB: I have. They're quite beautiful.

AS: Do you feel that your time with him contributed to his work?

RB: I'm sure it has, somehow.

AS: He never played in a band again after your breakup.

RB: Not seriously, anyway. Remember that our breakup wasn't long after Stonecipher came back from their only tour. He poured his heart and soul into that band. They were his first. I think it was easier for him to compose on his own afterwards than to risk being let down again.

AS: Let down how?

RB: By someone else not meeting his expectations.

AS: Aside from this feeling of groundlessness you mentioned, you hinted at how Reese was very determined to pursue his art.

RB: That's right.

AS: Did this determination get in the way of the relationship?

RB: We are two very strong, driven people with definite ideas about what we wanted to do. We were the same during our time together.

AS: So do you feel—

RB: None of this is news.

AS: What do you mean?

RB: I have repeated the same few statements to the press for years now. Years. I understand that you're doing your job. Many journalists I've talked to have poked our relationship with a stick. These questions you're asking are part and parcel of the interview process at this point. Each of you wants to be the one to get me to open up. Think of the prestige that would come with getting me to disclose why we stopped living together. You'd be famous. I don't blame you for trying. I'm getting older. There isn't much time left for me to reveal all my secrets. But I have no interest in doing so.

AS: I'm sorry.

RB: There's no need to be sorry. I understand that you're doing your job the best you can. But all of what I'm saying here has been said before.

○ ○ ○

(Freedom Springs Bugle, 12/12/2007. Used with permission.)

ANARCHIST DEMONSTRATION TURNS VIOLENT
by George McDonald, *Bugle* Staff

REPRESENTATIVES FROM THE MILITANT INDIGENEOUS Land Liberation Front have claimed responsibility for flipping a vehicle in Freedom Springs' financial district yesterday.

Eyewitnesses report that a clear moving van, decorated with plastic trees to portray the rainforest, was attacked by sign- and projectile-wielding activists dressed identically in black, wearing skimasks.

Via email, ILLF spokesperson hAkiM M@zZta pR0teXXXa[46] stated that "TROPIKKKAL (sic) NUT MUNCH IS A NEFARIOUS MULTINATIONAL CONGLOMERATE DECIMATING THE RAINFOREST FOR PROFIT$. WE ACCEPT FULL RESPONSIBILITY FOR THE DESTRUCTION OF THEIR FACIST MARKETING DEVICE."

Richard Johnson, of InTempts Staffing and Freedom Springs liason to Fastor, owner of Tropical Nut Munch brand, said that the ILLF's accusations are "completely groundless." When reached over the phone, Johnson praised Fastor's hiring policies as "progressive" and "innovative," citing the implementation of live actors in the promotion of their product as "a bridge to the future."

In the past, Fastor has come under fire for disobeying environmental policies, and for moving their factories to countries lacking strict child labor laws.

The ILLF also claimed responsibility for organizing WTO protests[47] in Seattle.

An unidentified employee of Tropical Nut Munch was in the truck when it was flipped. He escaped without serious injury and declined hospital care.

○ ○ ○

I WENT TO THE STORE TODAY TO BUY NOODLES AND
BOK CHOY. THERE WAS AN AMBULANCE IN PARKED IN
FRONT. I SAW A BODY BEING LOADED IN. IT WAS HIM. THE
EMT TOLD ME THE MAN DRANK HIMSELF TO DEATH. I
TOLD HIM TO BUY FOOD WITH THAT MONEY. IF I BOUGHT
HIM FOOD MYSELF, HE MIGHT NOT HAVE DIED.

○ ○ ○

So THAT TIME WHEN YOU came down—
  Max.
  Fuck.
  Sorry *Bernie* came down to see me I couldn't believe it he's always
chained to his desk so he took time off to come out pretty important
he asked if I wanted to go grab a beer is the Dingo open at two in the
afternoon it is he said wow man you must be pretty hardcore if you
know when it opens I was hoping he'd tell me about the artist girl
Rhonda they seemed like they were into each other at the opening
she didn't want anything to do with me can't blame a guy for trying
though but he said I want to talk business with you can I buy you a
beer. Beer! I appreciate the offer man but we can do it here it's too
early for me to drink besides I was out last night fair enough he said
taking pictures if I'm gonna be in that magazine I have to be out taking pictures so I can paint them sure he said I'm going to get some
coffee do you need anything I'm good he walked up to Cordelia she
poured him a big mug he came back listen man he said we're going on
tour to support our album. Yeah how's that going we've been working
on getting stuff set up Ben has been helping out with some places
around here you know Chicago Indy Toledo so I think they'll be okay
we'll get at least a little bit of the Dead Trend crowd but I'm not sure
how we'll do outside of the Midwest. How far are you going to
California and to Boston. Those are the two most faraway points.
That's awesome I know I can't wait just for the adventure you know
I've never traveled that much all these new cities when am I going to
have the chance to go to like Spokane again seriously I said that's
great Amy wants to hire a publicist to make sure there's people at all
the shows she thinks Dead Trend will help us draw even though she

wasn't in the band I said started laughing. Reunion, whatever! Exactly he said so she's been calling around looking for help they're all expensive like if we hire a publicist it's three hundred bucks a week or something like that Ben says he'll front us but he's already doing the records so I don't want to take any more money from him so I was wondering how much it would cost to have you do some of your blogging for our tour. I'd need to see a list I said how long are you gone for two months he said whoa that's a long tour he took a list of dates out of his pocket I've never done anything this big before I said I can do all my blogs and I'll give you a list of messageboards to hit I'll do the blogs for free that's easy the real work is the messageboards you do posting before you leave and I'll help while you're on the road what do you mean he said I don't know messageboards that's the way you can reach your audience that's how everyone knows about Faze post enough people start to believe you so you can do all that for free I can I said whether or not you decide you want to pay someone else to do it too okay he said I'll tell Amy.

So how's it going with Rhonda I said she's hot she seemed to like you we've got tough schedules he said but we've found time to hang out schedules I said like you have to pencil each other in. Perfect. You know he said does she keep hours like you well kinda I said she sleeps weird hours so it's hard but we're doing the best we can we like to see each other did you slip it to her yet I said Max he said come on no of course not he looked down I knew that he had good for you man I said.

I did not look down.

You so did I knew it right then.

○ ○ ○

ONE OF BEN'S OLD CHICAGO acquaintances, the former drummer of Californium Three, maintained an extensive list of club and booking contacts in and around the Midwest. Ben made calls and sent emails over the course of an afternoon, resulting in shows from Chicago through Louisville.

Amy's friend Seth did the brute work of cold calling. Ben guessed that his motivation was twofold: misguided chivalry mixed with the need for a new audience.

o o o

THE DINGO WAS QUIET WE were pretty much the only people there except for some factory workers playing pool me Bernie Amy this old guy Seth who I guess used to play drums in the original Dead Trend he didn't say much just kinda sat there smiled nodded his head a lot. They were all excited because they got records back from the plant Amy still had a courier bag from when they were hip in 1997 or whenever it was covered with one inch pins she put it up on the table opened the flap took out a copy. The cover was all grey like granite the word 'Stonecipher' across the top like it was carved into the rock I thought it looked heavy metal but still it was cool. The back cover was all black except for white words names of the songs their names a photo which Ben took when they played there that time I kicked some redneck's ass for talking shit about my jacket.

Wow I said that's fucking awesome you guys have a record out.

Jusht in time for tour Bernie said getting up they did the recording right after the show so they'd have something to give Lara Fox-Turner for the magazine which still wasn't out she said the next few weeks the last time I emailed her like a week ago. I didn't see Bernie for a while after that fucked up video where anarchists flipped the truck said he was staying in laying low but I think what he was really laying was pipe he didn't talk about that too much but Amy told me he moved all of his stuff out of Nine Northbrook they had to find a roommate some college kid moved in I guess she worked doubles so she could afford to pay rent while she was gone it was too cheap not to. Bernie did a little tour booking too but I guess the dude Seth helped Amy with most of it Bernie hit all the message-boards I told him to never posted links to the video like I told him to people if a band came to town and had some guy in it that was in a glass fan flipped by anarchists I'd totally go see that band people love shit like that but he wouldn't do it even though I told him to anyway Seth called clubs he remembered said he was in Dead Trend managed a new band with ex-members touring their debut LP released on vinyl.

Ben gave us three hundred of these puppies to sell on tour Amy said he's giving us tour support too. This is for you she said. Bernie came back to the table with four bottles of Venerable he didn't usually drink that much that was his third one already he was slurring his words a little he hadn't been drunk since his dad died I don't think I am sho happy he said that I am friendsh with all of you. I have been working hard to become a good drummer for yearsh now and I never thought I would tour or releash a record but I am. He gave everyone a beer and said Merry Chrishmash everyone.

Was I that bad?

Yeah.

○ ○ ○

MUCH HAS BEEN MADE OF Rhonda Barrett's failed cohabitation with Bernie Reese. Both were intensely guarded about their private lives. Save for Reese's journals, no substantial documentation of their time together exists.

The primary source material for the couple's cohabitation would have been Barrett's painting, but that second canvas is famously (and perhaps not coincidentally) damaged. Both Barrett and Reese have maintained that its destruction was accidental.

The first canvas's last dated entry is June 16, 2007, some three months before the opening of Hidden Wheel. The third canvas begins on April 1, 2008. It would appear, from the dates, that ten months of Barrett's work was destroyed, accidentally or otherwise. Oxford Melberg[48], among the first to tackle Barrett and her work, speculated that a period of domestic bliss lessened Barrett's workload. His meticulous research yielded what is commonly known as the Lines-Per-Month theory.

In addition to the dogged determination Barrett utilized in proving a lasting chronicle of her era, she did so in a consistent fashion, typically detailing her day in sixty to seventy words. Melberg's famous research states that Barrett's work typically consists of six lines per inch, with each line discussing somewhere between ten days and two weeks, depending on the length of the words she used.[49] A span of ten months, in a typical Barrett painting, would yield 3½ inches of text. On the second canvas, slightly more than an inch and a half of canvas was destroyed/obscured. Therefore, Melberg speculated, there were gaps, likely caused by a 'honeymoon period' in the relationship.

This theory was prevalent for almost fifty years, until Amanda Hanson's hypothesis that Barrett wrote and edited her work in a notebook during the Reese years, in an attempt not to incriminate or defame her domestic partner with her words. Hanson's theory has been dominant since its publication in 2117, based on the discovery of a notebook containing Barrett's final five entries, penciled and corrected, and a note stating that she had burned the notebook's multiple companions.

I remain skeptical. Why would Barrett burn all notebooks except for her final one, which contained such a note? Ever the consummate chess player, Barrett left us in check. She did not want us to know what happened in her shared loft, and left us a trap into which to fall. What if we suppose that the note is not true? What may have caused the painting to be destroyed?

○ ○ ○

OBSOLETE AT AGE SEVENTEEN. HARD DRIVE WIPED AND DOWNGRADED. INSTEAD OF PERFORMING HIGH TASKS I HAVE BECOME A SERIES OF PULLEYS LIFTING AND RELEASING. THE SPOTLIGHTS HAVE DIMMED. ALL THE STUDY FOR NAUGHT. THERE MUST BE SOMETHING ELSE. UNTIL I FIND IT THERE IS THIS UNLESS THIS IS ALL THERE IS. I DO NOT WANT TO WATCH OTHERS ROBBED AS I HAVE BEEN.

○ ○ ○

I GOT AN EMAIL FROM Derek today. He said a leave of absence would be fine—I can start again when I get back from tour.

I didn't tell Derek I'm going to stop a few weeks after I get back. Just enough donation to get back on my feet after tour, then I'm done.

○ ○ ○

AT CAFFIEND SITTING THERE LOOKING out the window when I saw him walk past I'm not going to chase the guy or anything like that. I assumed it was a fight. I never saw anyone rock it out though so I decided to take it to go with my next look really well I knew I needed something because Lara Fox-Turner said any day which meant everyone was going to bite my shit again like they did with Velcro with gas station before that pacifiers rave thing. I loved those. Pacifiers. Those are old though I needed something new I couldn't think of anything all these satin jackets like jocks used to wear with flared pants some of them so big they're practically bell-bottoms that's what it was for a while I couldn't think of anything else but needed something no one had done satin yet. That could be me. I could be first in satin. But I wasn't feeling it. I saw everyone sold their flares back when prestressed jeans came out so I figured I was safe everyone was wearing those v-cut shirts too so regular seemed like a safe bet really cheap the thing is though or was I should say that so what? I had this look which was kinda seventies kinda disco but who the fuck cares the seventies happened it's not like this is anything new but I couldn't get it together it was forced. I wasn't feeling it. I wanted to but I wasn't. So I thought I might as well had these suits made down at the tailor zoot suits so fucking cool big hats with feathers on them long coat really bright colors they cost a ton but I was like who the fuck cares twenty suits is nothing money coming in paintings the magazine coming out hard not to wear them until the magazine but fishing was still mine then that guy walked by I was like perfect I won't just be some retro I'm going to be commenting on it all the time like my work which comments on the demise of purchased media in an age surrounded by a mist of dissolving commerce that's what I was going to tell the next person who wanted to interview me I'd been working on it every night Lara Fox-Turner said I had to present a cogent reading of my work I thought it's going to hurt probably pretty fucking bad but I can make that part of my thing like who helped me accessorize that week like an autograph in reverse.

So I went over to Cordelia she'd been really nice since all the paintings sold months ago like in the space of two weeks gone one or two a day I said Cordelia she said what I said I want you to punch me in the face as hard as you can. Pow! She put down the espresso baton and said what in the world would you want me to do that for because I'm an artist I said. I have a vision. Which side do you think a black eye would look better on?

○ ○ ○

(From Freedom Springs Bugle, 1/1/2008. Used with permission.)

STONECIPHER: S/T
FRANCIUM HOTELIER, BUGLE STAFF

IT'S SAFE TO SAY THAT Freedom Springs has never seen, or heard, anything quite like Stonecipher. That much should be obvious from the first moment your needle hits the record (yes, record. Vinyl is back, and it's bigger than ever): Dead Trend alum Amy Czjdeki's basslines rumble like digestion as drummer Bernie Reese eschews timekeeping in favor of playing an endless pattern of creatively primitive fills. Czjdeki doubles as the band's singer, spitting angry nonsense at random.

Never mind the fact that it sounds, initially (and, to be fair, even after several listens), as if the two members of the band are playing in separate rooms, with no awareness of one another. And never mind seemingly misplaced signifiers—the cover of the album, bearing the band's name carved into granite, evokes mid-eighties metal. What lies at the heart of Stonecipher's jumble is an honesty so pure that it's almost pitiable—Czjdeki isn't a people person, she tells us, can't stand secretaries, nurses, rollerbladers. The band communicates their alienation and depression with modern life in the only way they know how. There's no way this record is ever going to sell—I wouldn't be surprised if the band carried boxes of the album from group house to group house for the next ten years, maybe more[50]—but that's part of the intrigue. This record is no joke, no novelty, no puzzle for the sake of it. And unlike much of what's being played on the radio today, it *bears repeated listens.* Reese's drumbeats stutter and pause, obviously linked to something—but what? What are the band's cues?

Seeing them live sheds no new light on the mystery—they bash and scrape as they stare straight at each other without a tic of recognition or theatrics. What you see (or hear, in this case) is what you get, an unnamable experience unambiguous in its presentation but completely baffling in its execution. I get the sense that Stonecipher is playing this music because they *have* to—there's no phony platform or mission statement, merely a grey backdrop, from which they chip away with grim aplomb. Maybe attention should be paid to the chips they let drop—melody, harmony, straight drumbeats—or maybe the monstrosity they render with their broad strokes *is* the sculpture, after all. Either way, as Czjdeki's borborygmal basslines suggest, this is a hard one to digest. But with the economy the way it is, sometimes the hardest stuff to swallow is the most filling.

Stonecipher is embarking on a full U.S. tour in support of their album. They return to Freedom Springs in March to play with Brooklyn's God Fires Man at Hidden Wheel Art Gallery.

o o o

THE LADY WHO TOOK MY picture looked like she'd been doing it for years I always wondered who the people were who went around to high class parties to take pictures for the magazines all the sudden she's in my face as I'm being introduced to some banker by the host some woman who saw *ArtScene* then the article about me in the *Bugle*. I'm at the top of one of the skyscrapers downtown I thought it was an office building not some penthouse with marble floors the caterer poured me a beer into a plastic cup I couldn't remember the name of that pine tree drink from Hub Seven then she had me meet everyone saying this is the artist I was telling you about I wish I had cards everyone seems to have read the magazine or maybe just the *Bugle* the lady with the camera said smile flash! in her other hand went off then she asked what my name was I told her she said watch in the *Bugle* Sunday About Town section you might see your picture the editor loves when artists come to these things I was the youngest person there by about twenty years except for the staff in tuxedo shirts. Poor bastards. Walking around with silver trays these little pieces of food on them goat cheese and roast pepper crust teeny the first one said it sure is I said took one it tasted good then duck con fee whatever the hell fee is it sure tasted good anyway little napkins all these old fogeys came up asked about urban revitalization, gentrification all this stuff I had no idea about so I told them a bunch of bullshit they always laughed but I knew that they didn't think my jokes were funny so I started making worse jokes. Awful. Like dumb shit they kept laughing the whole time but I didn't think they knew I was doing that on purpose maybe that's what these things were like though I'd never been only went to two more after that one.

I told them all that my paintings were available through Hidden Wheel Gallery they didn't know where it was down in the warehouse district I said it's a gallery show space no one knew where it was this guy a doctor I think with those liver spots on his forehead asked who owned it I tell him Ben Wilfork the guy stopped for a second said of the Chicago Wilforks I thought about it for a second I'd heard Ben talk about Chicago a few times I think he might've gotten Stonecipher a show there I think he's from Chicago I said well the guy said it's no surprise that this young Ben is doing something interesting that family is always diversifying what do you mean I said diversifying some of those Chicago families are single-minded in their money the Throckwhipples have been a mustard family for years new bottles new marketing but mustard is mustard it's a solid industry now the Wilforks the guy said James Wilfork was one of the men who developed the patent for the compact disc William before him was key in the development in heating elements for electric ranges. Raymond before that was oil. I think it's interesting that this Ben is selling art, but he'll probably succeed that family's track record is just impeccable. I almost said he's selling weed, too but I didn't. Why would a guy who came from all this money be selling drugs it wasn't that day might not have been that week I can't remember exactly when but I figured it out he just did it to look cool I was like Ben is a fucking poser.

ooo

PHONE CALLS STARTED THE WEEK the magazines arrived in boxes on Hidden Wheel's doorstep. They were all the same: did the mosaicist have anything for sale? Ben had it written down on an index card at his desk: the numbered show editions had gone fast. A second batch, painted by the artist after the show, was available. These were important pieces, as the artist had changed his perspective.

Ben sold half of the unnumbered low batch at four hundred dollars per and wrote Max another check.

He sold the other half to Jen. I'll get you some money soon, she said. A few weeks later, he received a check with a note—an average of two thousand per. It's almost time for the numbereds, the note said.

He'd sell the Caffiend set after the numbereds sold out.

Unsolicited demos and portfolios began arriving the same week. He had expected some mail to arrive—Max, as usual, was busy online—but hadn't expected so much legitimate press (or, so much attention from the viral video). Max was hot, Rhonda's glacial anti-commercial, anti-photo stance was mysterious[51], Festival of Hamburgers' record was out, and Stonecipher's album continued to garner raves. It was more attention than he expected. Or really needed. He could easily have a show every night of the week, but then it wouldn't be fun any more—it would be a job. He might as well move back to Chicago.

Shows would mostly be Friday and Saturday nights. Plenty of time to travel.

Art, once every two months or so. Small, then big. Or maybe medium—polymers, plywood, concrete. Whatever it was.

○ Chapter Seven

1/7/2008

NASHVILLE, TN. THREE PAID TONIGHT. The only person in the room during our set was the soundman. Our only contact in Greensboro is the record store we're playing, so we're in another hotel.

We played great. When I was doing the fill intro on "Buenos Noches, Minty Hands" I doubledstroked the tom hits by accident. Sounded awesome. Amy picked up on it and doubled all of her strumming for the rest of her song. First it was "Chicken-Shaped Patty Meal" the other night, now this. We keep getting better.

But Amy is pissed. She's talking about Max not doing his job and leaving our asses blowing in the wind, and the magazine coming out late and fucking us over. I told her that Louisville was awesome, and Toledo, and Chicago. She said we shouldn't be playing shows to three people.

When I try to tell her it's our first tour, she says that people should know who we are. She was in Dead Trend, and I was in a viral video.

She started talking about money. How was she supposed to quit waiting tables if we were playing to three people in the middle of nowhere? Aim, I said, it's going to take years of doing this before there's any money to be made. We're a strange band. This is our first tour. We need to put down groundwork for the next time we come through. I told her to think about how many people will come see us the next time we're in Louisville, based on the show we had there the other night.

1/8/2008

GREENSBORO, NC. ANOTHER FREE RECORD store show tonight, at a store called Gate City Noise. Nice people there. They took us to a hot dog place for "the best veggie dogs in the state." Sauerkraut and onions on mine.

Another great set. We went into this break on "Gorilla Statue of Liberty" and came back into the chorus at the same time without talking about it. Without really looking at each other, honestly. We both just knew.

They passed a hat for us and we got $32. We sold three records. Some guy there told Amy he had been listening to our MP3's and she freaked out on him. She yelled that he should be *buying* records, not stealing them online. How was a band supposed to make a living if people weren't supporting them? The guy, big with red hair, had a record under his arm. He probably put money in the hat, too. We'll never play that place again.

We're staying in a house with a guy who used to run a fanzine called Slave. He told us about being in a Misfits cover band on Hallowe'en. I say "us," but I mostly mean me. Amy has been in a horrible mood all day, since she yelled at the kid. This guy we're staying with was at the show, and is friends with the guy she yelled at—I saw them talking—so I'm not sure why he even let us stay here.[52]

○ ○ ○

I WAS HOPING FOR YOUNGER but after all this talk about her husband leaving her she said enough about me let's talk about you your art somewhere private pulled me into the bathroom the marble floor must kill her knees.

○ ○ ○

(Excerpted from ArtScene *magazine/pulsestream 29.6, August 2037. Used with permission.)*

ARTSCENE: You were remarkably canny with your investments.

RHONDA BARRETT: I was very fortunate to make as much money as I did. I took chances, and some paid off.

AS: How did you decide which companies to invest in?

RB: I am not at liberty to discuss where my money came from.

AS: Insider trading?

RB: Next question.

AS: It's probably been thirty years since you made your investments.

RB: I have no interest in incriminating anyone. Please. Is there another question?

AS: Using information like that for your own profit?

RB: I should mention that it wasn't for my profit at all. After I graduated high school, I didn't have a vacation for at least twenty years. I lived modestly—

AS: From what I can see, you still do.

RB: —I still do, yes—and delivered bread to restaurants. That money was most of my rent. All of my investments went into the Centers. I prefer to think of all the good I've done rather than focusing on the ethics of my cash flow.

AS: It's very Robin Hood.

RB: You're not the first person to mention that. (laughs) Except in my case there is not theft involved. I provided a service, and used the excess money to provide others. If businessmen hadn't paid me to abuse them, they likely would have found someone else. Where would that money have gone? Maybe into something good. A thousand dollars was a lot of money. It still is. Perhaps another woman in my line of work would have produced art or founded a charitable cause.

Or maybe not. Maybe all that money would have gone right up another woman's nose, or into her arm. It's horribly depressing work. There were periods when I wished my path was more traditional. But the work found me and allowed me to make a living and help others. Those dark periods are a small price to pay for doing so much good.

AS: How did you decide to begin?

RB: As you know, I played chess when I was younger.

AS: And you were very good.

RB: I was. I lost my passion for the game when Alexi Zaitsev was defeated in tournament play by Bigger Pink. I wanted to be the one to defeat Zaitsev.

AS: Do you think you could've beaten him?

RB: Having a chance to play him would've meant the stars aligning in a very specific way. I might've had a chance if I'd kept playing at a very high level. As far as beating him goes, who knows? Pundits call him the best player in the history of chess. It's very flattering to think of myself in that light, but it's likely that it was nothing more than wishful thinking on my part.

Even if it was just a pipe dream, I had a goal. I was working towards something. Having goals that are unreachable can be discouraging, but in some ways can be great. If Bigger Pink hadn't been built, I might still be playing towards Zaitsev.

AS: How would that be great?

RB: The process can be just as good as the results. My painting, for example, will never be finished until I'm dead. Those are the parameters of the project—to document my life in a very specific way. I have never taken the time to admire my work as a whole because it's not finished. And I'm not likely to, either. There may be a few minutes before I die when I concede that my life is ending, but I'll probably be worried about other things than my paintings at that point. (laughs)

But the *process* of painting has sustained me, just as chess did when I was younger. Young people have been moving away from the process—

AS: Which one?

RB: *Any* one, to more disposable things. We're fed information in bite-sized bits now, and encouraged to partake in activities which aren't rewarding or connecting. Videogames are a big one. There's certainly a process, but the game ends and the player is left with nothing.

AS: There are many games available online in which players build characters for years. DungeonQuest comes to mind. They build communities, too.

RB: There is a process to that, I suppose, but it's a process with no results. What if the main DungeonQuest computer crashed?

AS: I'm sure it's a series of—

RB: Theoretically. What would happen if it crashed?

AS: Everyone would lose their characters.

RB: They'd have nothing to show for their process. I understand that people derive enjoyment from playing such games, and they interact with people in a specific way online, but there's no feeling of community in playing a videogame. Everyone is an avatar of themselves. And multi-user online games like DungeonQuest may have process, but it's not a tangible sort. There are no real skills being developed. It's all in a world in a computer. Contributing to our obsolescence.

During my time playing chess at Le Petit Chapeau I wasn't struck by the sense of community those men and women had. I was too young to really notice it. In retrospect, it was like a family. They accepted me for who I was in a very real way. So my first thought was to encourage community and process. Initially, I thought I could affect the world around me in very small ways.

AS: Such as?

RB: I volunteered at a food bank. I gave money to the homeless.

AS: Why did you stop?

RB: A homeless man I gave money to drank himself to death. I started saving for my first Center afterwards—Chess. I lost money too quickly. (laughter)

AS: There's nothing tangible about chess games.

RB: Aside from records of the games, you're right. I liked the process of young people getting better at chess, and the community, but I wanted there to be tangible results, too. My second attempt was better.

○ ○ ○

HIS RESEARCH SUGGESTED THAT PITTSBURGH might be next. It was angry and affordable. Plenty of space. Not too much crime. Easily accessible.

He liked the people he met and the bands and art he saw. The spaces he toured were full of hip decay.

But it didn't feel right. It might've done in a pinch, but there was none. He'd keep looking.

○ ○ ○

MALE VOICE[53]: At first I was, you know, a little weirded out by it. I mean, I had never heard of any of it for real. You hear stories about crazy shit on tour or at school or whatever, videos online, but it's never like, you know, real. And this was.

I stopped asking questions after a while because I didn't want to know. But there was this big gap, you know, like 'how was your day at work?' That sort of thing. I tried to be cool with it because she thought it out so well, plus the novelty of it. I mean, it's kinda hot. (laughs) So that was a big part of it.

I, you know, assumed there would be spaces in the relationship, at least for a while. Where we agreed not to talk about certain things. Which was a mistake.

○ ○ ○

BEN KEPT ASKING ME FOR more paintings Cordelia too I thought about buying CD's just for the cases before Ben told me maybe WFSU[54] might be able to help me out he knew some people there I went down asked if they had any CD's they didn't want some guy with a beard wearing a flannel shirt there said are you kidding we have more than we know what to do with took me to this room full of CD's records I looked at them alphabetized he said this pile here is all extra pointed to boxes full of CD's take what you want he said we can't give these things away usually I said started filling my duffel bag can I come back the guy laughed we're happy for the space he said come as much as you want.

I shoved CD's into the bag then this kid came in wearing a fishing vest carrying a fishing rod this woven kinda bag like old men put fish in why hadn't I thought of that he had all these lures on his hat fishing vest plus knee boots I never had those the kid was good I wanted to give him a bunch of shit for ripping me off hey I wanted to say I invented that look don't you know who I am except he made me better I can respect that I mean my zoot suit is awesome no one's doing it but I bought it hey I said you look good he looked at me for a second that's a cool black eye did it hurt like a motherfucker I said we both started laughing listen he said that's a good look man what's it called again zoot suit I said that's right I like it but you've gotta get on this fishing thing or if you don't like fishing I've heard that some guys are dressing like hunters bright orange cowboy hats and shit the accessories are better with fishing you can't carry a gun around if you're a hunter because people will think you're a terrorist or something but still.

Thanks I said no sweat the kid said he walked into the rows of music to look for records I guess I couldn't remember feeling that sad for a long time maybe ever the kid has some good ideas the knee boots especially looked good the fish bag people were going to give him a lot of shit for carrying a purse but maybe not like the factory workers at the Dingo I beat up that time maybe they would have thought that he was coming back from fishing even though it was winter ice fishing maybe I don't know if people have lures on their hats and tackleboxes I should've checked that before I started that was my look first probably my best one I saw the way that gas station caught on everyone looks good in that but it was never hard to find any of that stuff jackets or shirts it became common so fast that people forgot that it was my thing first but the fishing that day I saw the guy walking down the street that was mine I got that first I thought of that everyone knew that I did I got my picture in a bunch of fucking magazines wearing that gear then some kid did me better than I ever could if I had stuck to it people might know they'd be like that's the artist he's the first guy to wear the fisherman look but instead I was some asshole with a black eye wearing custom suits I didn't even like them I just did it because Lara Fox-Turner told me it would be a good idea to reinvent myself. I didn't want to wear this shit any more I'm going to go back to being myself a fisherman.

○ ○ ○

1/17/2008

NEW YORK CITY. WE'RE ACROSS the river in Williamsburg right now, staying with Joe, one of the guys from God Fires Man. He came to the show tonight and told us that he was going to be playing Freedom Springs with us in March. He has a nice place. I'm on his couch. Amy is across the street at this bar Charleston that serves free pizza.

I had never been to ABC No Rio before, but I knew it was an important place that started off as a squat. Born Against used to play there, Rorschach, 1.6 Band. I don't know what Amy was expecting, exactly, but it wasn't a smelly basement. It looked full because it's so small, but that didn't improve her mood any. There were even some kids there wearing Dead Trend shirts, which didn't change things, either. When we loaded in she started calling me an asshole for booking a New York City show in a slum. She said she played a packed Bowery Ballroom last time. But the set was great, again. We tripled the beat on "Patty." I thought I'd lose the beat, but I stopped thinking and let my limbs take over. I want to record all the songs again to document the changes.

We sold four records and got paid ninety dollars, but she was still in a terrible mood. After the matinee Joe managed to squeeze into the passenger seat with Amy and he gave us directions to his place. We unloaded our gear into his entryway. Amy went straight to the bar and has been there since.

Joe took me on a walk around the neighborhood. He had to work, at the wine shop downstairs from his house, so he gave me his keys and told me to make myself at home. I've been watching DVD's for a while.

I called Rhonda. She asked if I thought we'd finish the tour. I told her I hadn't thought about it.

1/18/2008

FORT THUNDER CALLED. THEY'RE HAVING electrical trouble. The show today is cancelled.

Joe says we're welcome to stay at his place for another night. He says he can help out in Boston—he used to live there and knows people we could stay with. He does a lot of his recording at the studio up there where the album was mastered.

Once Amy wakes up I'll talk to her.

1/19/2008

CAMBRIDGE, MA. WE'RE IN A house in the Boston University neighborhood.[55] I tried to play a weird drinking game with the guys who live here, but it was too hard to follow. Something about making up new band names and voting on them. I'm on the couch with a friendly cat who keeps headbutting me.

We drove up yesterday. Amy had a huge whiskey hangover. She complained about her headache until Connecticut. I told her she was giving me a headache. She sulked for the rest of the drive.

First we went to New Alliance, down the street from the club we played at tonight, Middle East. The New Alliance space used to be a garage. There's a full recording studio there, practice spaces, and mastering. We met Rob, who mastered our record. Nice guy.

The New Alliance guys took us to the house we're staying at. We were going to stay at Rob's, but Amy bought a bottle of whiskey, drank a quarter of it and passed out on the couch. Mike, who lives here, doesn't seem to mind. He says that once someone pissed himself sleeping on a chair. Another time someone threw himself down the back stairs twice at the same party. Passing out is low impact, he said.

Everyone at the house has seen the video of me and the anarchists. They acted like I was famous, asking all these questions about how it had been staged. I told them it hadn't been. They showed me a video that had been shot from inside the PES. It must've been the corner camera in the fake trees. No one could believe that I hadn't seen that footage, or that I had been afraid for my life when the skimasks started trying to flip the PES. This one guy, Ed, says that I'm cool, but that doesn't mean I can lie to everyone about it. I think I managed to convince them I hadn't known the skimasks were coming. I told them about the misspelled signs and the tomatoes and four hours a day of fifteen-second dramatic persuasions. Mike thinks I should write an article about it. Ed doesn't think anyone would believe it. I'm not sure I can believe that footage leaked to the internet.

Amy was in a good mood today. The sun was out. Mike and Travis, the British guy who lives here, said it was pretty warm for Boston winter and took us on a walk around town, up through the Jewish neighborhood and into the city. We walked around the shopping district all the way to the Boston Common, which is a big park in the middle of the city where sheep used to graze. From there we walked up the river back to their neighborhood.

The people at Middle East fed us falafel before the show. We opened for a three-piece named Ketman, who reminded me of a modern Minutemen. Everyone in the band was great, the drummer especially. I talked to her for a little while after the show.

Tonight was the tightest we've been since Louisville. Amy was screaming her head off for the entire set and kicked her amp over at the end. Rockstar. Ninety dollars tonight, and two records sold (I traded one with Ketman, too).

We have a day off tomorrow, then Buffalo. Ed says it's at least nine hours. We'll get up late and see how we feel. Unless Amy shows up in the next few minutes I'm going to sleep right here on this couch with this cat.

1/20/2008

AMY WAS ASLEEP NEXT TO the couch when I woke up. I got dressed and found a bagel place for breakfast.

When I got back, she was awake, pacing the length of the house.

I think I knew right then.

Listen, she said. This isn't what I thought it was going to be at all. I'm really unhappy. I've been trying to make the best of it, but I can't stand this. I want to go home.

I asked her if we could play the rest of the shows. She said she couldn't handle another day.

I don't know what else to say.

○ ○ ○

WHAT LEO SAID YOU CAN'T afford it even though you're selling all those paintings come on man I said it's not about that getting back to your roots that's right trying to keep it real hey he said didn't I see you wearing a yellow suit last week it was just a joke I said listen can I get some paint or what all right man wait a few minutes I'll be there so I went out back there was another guy hanging around too dressed as me waist-high boots tacklebox the whole deal the back door opened this woman I didn't know opened the door she had a plastic bag in her hand he went over took the bag it looked heavy I stood around for a few minutes before Leo came to the door here you go he said thanks dude no sweat I walked down the alley and onto the street stupid can't believe I threw the other ones away looked in pink green horrible but I guess they'd have to do. They were free.

○ ○ ○

CHESS CAN'T BE THE FOCUS. EVEN IF I TEACH CHILDREN HOW TO PLAY, THE INEVITABLE URGE TO DEFEAT A COMPUTER AS A SHOW OF SKILL STILL CONTRIBUTES TO OUR OBSOLECENSE. THE PROCESSES OF PAINTING AND WRITING WILL BEGET THE PROCESSES OF VIEWING AND READING INSTEAD. THE BEATINGS WILL CONTINUE UNTIL INTEREST RATES IMPROVE. YEARS TO GO.

○ ○ ○

COXSWAIN WAS DELIGHTED.[56] THEY SIGNED the paperwork in his office, servers humming behind.

We'll make some changes, he said. First, we're going to print some CD's, for radio airplay. I was under the mistaken impression that radio stations still played records. It appears, based on the CMJ numbers, that they do not. Airplay certainly would have helped Stonecipher stay together. I'll do an extra fifty beyond the radio batch. You can do with them what you wish.

Second: I want you to do small local tours first. Stonecipher may have been too ambitious in their itinerary. Chicago, Indianapolis, Louisville. The arts center in Toledo. Some of you did two full U.S. tours with Pee Valves. You know how audiences are.

○ ○ ○

Every day I wake up paint the pictures from the night before while I drink coffee take ibuprofen I head over to Caffiend after then work on business. Ben keeps giving me checks the paintings are moving he says he's working on a big deal to get thirty of them into the same gallery when I'm not working on the gallery or Stonecipher at viral websites I hype myself conduct interviews with myself I'm a very good interview I think I have ideas about the state of commodities shit like that I link to the piece in the Bugle I wish I could link to the parties I get invited to they'd be like this guy's for real man he's got mad bitches to all the kids who dress like me to everyone who bought one of my paintings.

Caffiend slows down I'm like that's cool my real audience is down at the art gallery all the rich in-the-know peeps go there for their art needs Ben tells me he's getting a new exhibit ready there's some woman builds sculptures out of driftwood old computer chips she calls them colonies.

○ ○ ○

(*"Ten Years On."* ArtScene, *November 2017. Reprinted with permission.*)

ArtScene: It's been ten years for both of us.

Benjamin Wilfork: Closer to eleven for you, I believe.

AS: That's right, Benjamin. I'll always be older. (laughter)

BW: Don't you forget it.

AS: Now, ten years after the opening of your Hidden Wheel art gallery, are you surprised by your success?

BW: It had very little to do with me. The quality of the art was pure. Freedom Springs is a special place. Maybe it's something in the air. Or the water.

AS: Festival of Hamburgers are one of the biggest bands in the world. Did you have any idea?

BW: I wish I had. It doesn't surprise me that much—some of the members were in a Freedom Springs band called Pee Valves, who I liked a great deal. The other members went on to be in Coxswain, of course, who have done very well for themselves. I'm proud to be involved in their first four albums. Bernie Reese, who played in Stonecipher, is hard at work recording what he calls another percussive symphony.

AS: Your first show set a standard for art: small, fast pieces.

BW: That's right. Mizst, known also as Max Caughin, god rest his soul, was doing great work with CD cases at a time when the music industry was becoming very fractured. I thought, moving forward, that Hidden Wheel's focus should be contemporary work by emerging artists using the newest medium. The very next show was the debut of Franzia Levah, whose work incorporated microchips in a nature setting. Erick Hoffnagel's rotary phone work was after that.

AS: You have consistently been on the lookout for new mediums for expression. How do you respond to critics who say that your gallery breeds nine-day wonders?

BW: It's jealousy. Festival of Hamburgers played at my gallery. Franzia Levah got her start with me, Janine O'Day, Adrien Komp. Artists who are receptive to the world around them, who strive to constantly reinvent themselves.

○ ○ ○

AMY CAME OVER YESTERDAY AND dropped off my kit. She told me she wouldn't mind playing shows now and again. I told her it had to be all or nothing. She said she understands. And she apologized to me.

All her talk about Dead Trend didn't match up to what was in my head. I guess I hoped maybe we'd be driving around in busses someday, playing in nice rooms. But I didn't mind floors and the hatchback.

The kit is in the corner behind the door. There's a huge echo around the room when I play. It sounds great.

I'm going to start making calls to see if anyone wants to play with me. Rhonda says she doesn't mind. That's because she hasn't been here while I've been playing. I won't blame her if she changes her mind.

Donation today. Ten left, before taxes, until I get my balance paid down.

○ ○ ○

BODY FOUND IN DITCH REMAINS UNIDENTIFIED
James Fern, *Bugle* staff

A BADLY MUTILATED BODY DISCOVERED outside of Duncan remains unidentified, according to DPD chief Hal Woolf.

According to Woolf, forensics experts have determined the body fell from some height before being dragged behind a large vehicle, presumably an 18-wheeler.

"We're going to dental records next," Woolf said.

The body was found in a ditch by work-release prisoners on Tuesday.

○ Chapter Eight

I've been watching my bank account, thinking maybe CC would direct deposit. They haven't. I called them today. They said that if the check hadn't arrived already, it would soon.

○ ○ ○

I WAS AT CAFFIEND WORKING on my third cup when a delivery guy came I didn't recognize Cordelia signed the guy dumped three big boxes off the handtruck Cordelia opened one the new issue of *ArtScene* she said I opened one read it didn't see anything about myself or Hidden Wheel but put one in my tacklebox for later.

○ ○ ○

LEWIS BRINKMAN: She always seemed happy, until Zaitsev happened. Her mom dying, obviously—that was a blow, but when she returned she seemed the same. Same Rhonda. Then Zaitsev.

That's when she took on the world. And she's doing well, from what I see. (laughter) But I wonder if her painting, her charity made her happy. Did she seem happy to you? When you lived with her?

BERNIE REESE: Yes.[57]

LEWIS BRINKMAN: Was she painting?

BERNIE REESE: No. No she wasn't. Not at all.

○ ○ ○

STONECIPHER DISBANDED WITHIN DAYS OF the Freedom Springs issue's release.

Jen told him she'd be happy to write a follow-up piece. A romantic spin on the pressures of a young band on the road would go over well, she said. Plus, a sidebar on the drummer's reaction to his viral appearance, maybe interspersed with coverage of the performance artist collective responsible for flipping the truck.

Too much, Ben said. Too soon.

Franzia Levah was in the process of finishing pieces for her exhibit. Two months was their goal. Coverage of her gallery opening would add cache. And it looked as if Coxswain's debut LP would be ready at roughly the same time.

○ ○ ○

RHONDA GOT UP EARLY SO Louis and I could have the place to ourselves. She told me it was important to feel like we had space the first time. She went to get breakfast at the diner.

Louis came over and set up his amp and guitar in the outlet next to my desk. I was excited—as long as I've known him he's played bass. He told me he was a guitarist first.

He stepped on Rhonda's painting when he was tuning. I forgot how much of a pacer he is. She told me it was cool if there were marks on the canvas, but he started walking back and forth when he put on his guitar. I thought it was too much.

I told him to stop for a minute and rolled up the empty canvas to make more floorspace. I made sure to stop rolling before I got to the part where Rhonda was working.

We played for an hour or so. There were probably twenty good minutes, where we locked in. His tone is trebly, which he says is a political statement.

We decided to play next week, same time. Louis broke down his gear and left.

After he left is when I noticed.

Rhonda's painting, the part that she had been working on, fell off the wall. I unrolled the canvas to see if it was okay.

The newest work she did, last week, smudged onto some earlier lines. Some of it is unreadable.[58]

She came back half an hour after Louis left. I had never seen her get mad before.

I hoped she wouldn't freak out on me.

I told her I had rolled the canvas to give Louis more room to play and the painted part had fallen off the wall.

She flushed. I saw her bite her lip.

I don't think you should play here any more, Bernie, she said. I know that accidents happen. And it's okay. But maybe you and Louis should play in your space instead.

We didn't talk much for the rest of the night. She went to the bakery early.

○ ○ ○

THE PAINTINGS STACKED UP NO one is buying I asked Cordelia if I should cut the prices she said you'll look desperate I wasn't taking so many pictures at nighttime any more because once I was done at the Dingo I went home changed all black ninja shit went out with my gasmask bag full of Leo's free paint did pieces wrote my name some more except not Mizst not any more everyone knew who he was it's Faze on the underpasses the colors are wack but what could I do they were free I was broke I went over to the yard wrote burners the designs I did in my notebook for a week or it was windy so my fill got messed up but I thought it looked pretty good. The next day though someone posted on CanDo about how they saw one of Faze's early burners it totally sucked everyone loves that guy so much but he was a toy when he started just like the rest of us green and pink what the fuck shit looked terrible.

○ ○ ○

(Excerpted from ArtScene *magazine/pulsestream 29.6, August 2037. Used with permission.)*

ARTSCENE: When did you first know you'd be a philanthropist?

RHONDA BARRETT: I never thought of myself like that. I was painting, but that alone wasn't enough to make me forget about my work. It paid well, but it was hard. It took its toll on me. I needed an escape that my painting wasn't providing, biking wasn't. Giving some of the money away complicated things. I didn't know where the money was going.

When I established my first clinic, I felt like a weight had been lifted. There, finally, was a way for me to feel better. In addition to my work, providing the means for others to record their existences, through whatever means they liked, would help right the balance.

After a time, I found it easier to be more specific in my donations. The first one, in Freedom Springs, was perhaps a little too diverse (laughter). It was trying to be too many things to too many people. So I settled, finally, on painting. Then writing after that.

I was surprised, initially, by the amount of resistance. I suppose some of it had to do with my history. I think most of it was fear. Which is why I decided to cater to teens. So they could have an easier time than I did.

○ ○ ○

BAD NEWS BEN SAID ON the phone the deal fell through all the dealers buyers are saying the market is oversaturated with urban mosaicism I thought you were going to sell thirty of my paintings I said I was Ben said but the prevalent trends have fluctuated buyers have had their fill of urban mosaicism the speculative market is correcting itself what do you mean I said speculative the investment in futures Ben said is a major part of this business yours is not as bright as we had all hoped. What's the next thing I said maybe I can start working on something new it's hard to tell what the new market is going to be Ben said come on I said I know all about electric ranges oil CD's you fucking know my advice to you would be to research what's online if you want to stay up with contemporary trends or use your considerable blogosphere influence to steer things in your direction what about this new thing that's in the new *ArtScene* with all the plastics you've got the next one all figured out don't you I'll melt some CD cases down by the time you get started Ben said that trend will likely be over you know how these things go you may continue to carve a niche for yourself as an urban mosaicist after all you were Freedom Springs' major export in that genre you may have enough of a market to sustain a cottage industry until the inevitable revival fuck that I said I want the money to roll right in surely Ben said you saved some of that the parties all those douchebags with their caterers passing food around it would be a shame if it were all gone the kids the fishermen that was me that was mine now it's everywhere perhaps it's time you reassessed your position I saw some kid the other day I'm positive that black eye was because of me if there's anything I can help you with please let me know whether it's the usual or anything moving forward Faze is making a comeback new work has been unearthed it's time for his discovery we will talk soon.

○ ○ ○

(Excerpted from ArtScene *magazine/pulsestream 29.6, August 2037. Used with permission)*

ArtScene: Did you ever consider starting a family?

Rhonda Barrett: I don't know anyone raised in a single-parent household who wasn't fucked up in some very fundamental way.

AS: Weren't you?

RB: I rest my case. (laughter)

○ ○ ○

When I came back from Louis's space all my stuff was boxed up outside the door. A check from Central Cryonics sat right on top of the pile.

My key didn't work.

I called Rhonda.

You're not part of the solution, Bernie, she said.

I'm just doing it until I pay my balance, I said. I'm almost done. Or I can stop. I'll just stop right now.

I thought I knew you but I was wrong. Donating sperm? You're one of them. Goodbye.

○ ○ ○

I'M FUCKING AFRAID OF HEIGHTS all it'll take is one step a slip a second of forgetting because I get so into the pieces that I'll drop even though there are barely any cars plus the fog the drop alone would break something but it's the best. The best fucking place for it. Clipped through the fence everyone will see him the visibility will be better than any stupid magazine or bullshit webpage can give besides me telling you about it will protect me.

Is that all for today?

Can you think of anything else?

I think I told you everything.

⟳ Endnotes, Etc.

[1] Caughin's passages in this work have been presented as they were discovered. As no audio recordings of his voice exist, we must assume that Bernard Reese, in his transcription of these interview sessions, chose not to punctuate Caughin's words to preserve a rambling, run-on style of speech.

[2] Artificial plants, unironically thought to bring life to a room, were often found in offices and residences during the Early Millenia.

[3] Freedom Springs' pedestrian riverside path is the present-day site of Wilfork Towers.

[4] Records show that Crank's birthname was Francis Hopkins Farrington III. The Farringtons were well-known in real estate and steel circles.

[5] Common parlance for pre-portable talk-only telephones.

[6] An audio capture device of the sort mentioned in the introduction. The point Caughin seems to be making here is that the unexpected juxtaposition of two seemingly unrelated items is jarring at first, then commonplace after a time.

[7] One of *ArtScene* magazine's Lara Fox-Turner's most publicized regrets was that she had not attended the show, which she referred to as "the beginning of Freedom Springs as we know It."

[8] This long interview, with a retired Lara Fox-Turner of *ArtScene*, is the only existing conversation with Barrett. Prior to the Datastrophe, Barrett, tight-lipped though she was, spoke with other journalists and scholars—Oxford Melberg's and Amanda Hansons's respective books contain direct quotes from interview sessions, as does Cheryl Kearns' "American Charge"—but the source materials have been lost.

[9] Barrett's pre-art chess visions were the subject of speculation for years prior to this interview.

[10] Similar to the compact disc, which held sound recordings, the DVD, or digital video disc, was a commercially available medium on which motion pictures and their accompanying audio were stored and played.

[11] Karaoke was largely an amateur pursuit in the early 21st century.

[12] A legendary Chicago music club.

[13] Cheryl Kearns speculates in "American Charge" that Freedom Springs was not Wilfork's first choice of locales. Despite his affluence, she postulates, startup costs were prohibitively expensive in every locale but Freedom Springs.

[14] Typically, compact disc cases were nearly square in shape, to replicate the look of record albums sleeves. The front panel was typically clear and contained an insert detailing band members, recording information, etc. DVD's, however, were longer, rectangular, and opaque.

[15] The Barrett Trust's stringent rules regarding citation and reproduction of Rhonda Barrett's six canvases prevent me from depicting this passage (indeed, any passage herein from her canvases) in its full splendor. What is often lost in discussions of Barrett's steadfast devotion to her aesthetic vision and artistic regiment is the beauty of her work. The brushstrokes in this particular passage are immaculate: with a precision which seems otherworldly, Barrett rendered her daily offering with confidence and grace for which words do no justice. After years, I cannot even begin to approach the fastidious elegance of Barrett's small, strong lines and letters.

I encourage you—indeed, everyone—to visit any of the six Barrett Stalwart Trust Centers, in Freedom Springs, New York, Chicago, Houston, Seattle or Atlanta, so as to witness Barrett's multi-faceted genius in person. There really is no substitute.

[16] At the beginning of the 21st century, one hundred terabytes was enough space to save the sum total of human knowledge several times over.

[17] This first human-computer chess match was held in the last decade of the 20th century, some forty years before the advent of the All-Robot Olympics.

[18] Lara Fox-Turner, nee Jennifer Fishton, met Ben Wilfork while both were in Chicago. I am pleased to say that Fishton/Turner attended Freedom Springs University in her late teens. It is speculated, in "American Charge," that Benjamin Wilfork relocated to Freedom Springs on Fishton/Turner's advice.

[10] In the latter 20th and early 21st centuries, fringe groups speculated that computer power would render humans obsolete. The moment of human obsolescence was to be known as the Singularity. One can only wonder what such fringe groups (and Rhonda Barrett, whose fear was chess-based, and, I think, valid under her own set of circumstances) would think of the Datastrophe.

[20] Despite providing free food to members of the Freedom Springs art and music scenes, Fogtown Burrito was known as a haven for unhygienic food service practices.

[21] It is easy to forget that primitive Early Milennial devices utilize the same binary base as our present-day technology.

[22] The full Dead Trend lineup roster:
I. 1986–1988: Gil Falcone *(vocals)*, Mike Roft *(guitar)*, Marty Haratt *(bass)* Seth Stina *(drums)*
II. 1988–1989: Falcone, Roft, Stu Barone *(bass)*, Stina
III. 1989–1995: Falcone, Roft, Denny Stairstep *(bass)*, John Alcidez *(drums)*
IV. 1995: Falcone, Roft, Mark O'Meara *(second guitar)*, Nate Popov *(bass)*, John Cantone *(drums)*
V. 1996–1997: Falcone *(vocals, guitar)*, O'Meara *(guitar, vocals)*, Lou Shutt *(bass)*, Freddy DeSantine (drums)
VI. Reunion: Falcone, O'Meara, Amy Czjdeki *(bass)*, DeSantine

[23] Barrett's plight, here rendered, once again, in beautiful, strong strokes the Barrett Trust will not allow me to reproduce photographically, is typical of Early Millennial pre-All Access Amendment gender values.

[24] Caughin here transfers money from one online commerce system to another through a proxy account set up in Dubai, a city later razed in favor of silicon and alkaline mining. Dubai, like the former American city of Las Vegas, was based on the premise of conspicuous consumption, and, as such, had very lax monetary regulatory principles.

[25] History repeats itself.

[26] The prevalent digital format for many years, and a direct precursor to MP27's.

[27] Popular mid-20th century jazz musician known for off-time performances.

[28] Barrett biographers Oxford Melberg and Amanda Hanson both cite—correctly, I believe—Lara Fox-Turner's ability to seek out and recognize talent. Despite Reese's reluctance in this passage to accept Fox-Turner's statements, the fact remains that the Freedom Springs art and music scenes have her to thank for bringing their work to a larger audience.

[29] Barrett's paintings reveal initial musings on opening what would become Barrett Stalwart Trust Centers, though no documentation has been found to pin down a definitive date of origin. Oxford Melberg and Amanda Hanson's respective biographies of Barrett corroborate this point.

[30] Portable data storage devices for personal computers.

[31] Global Positioning Systems were early ancestors of WorldGrid ID's.

[32] The following is a transcription of an interview discovered on a compact disc among Bernard Reese's effects. I assume that Reese's voice is the first, even though its pitch was much lower than I had originally thought.

[33] Several instances of Ben Wilfork writing himself into history are documented, both in Cheryl Kearns' "American Charge" and in Sidd Kraves' short but impressive article on Max Caughin. His alleged attendance at the aforementioned Dead Trend show has been disproven by travel documents, which put Wilfork in Paris on that very day.

[34] An artist in Early Millenial Freedom Springs, before taxes, could live frugally on $20,000 for between a year and two years.

[35] Computer image files.

[36] Popular men's fantasy magazines.

[37] This is among the largest entries Barrett ever made, twice the length of an average passage. The Barrett Trust charges by the passage, rather than by the word, for reprint rights, so this excerpt, one of only a handful I could afford (despite my publisher's generous advance), is quite a value.

[38] Google, initially an online search engine, branched out into personal data storage, pulsestreaming and global positioning software before reorganization and subsequent overhaul into what we now know as WorldGrid.

[39] This passage is a continuation of the previous interview discovered on compact disc.

[40] Rainforests were thick accumulations of tropical vegetation.

[41] In a 2028 interview with a young Oxford Melberg, Barrett stated that her retirement, some five years earlier, came at a time when her clients were 'out of harm's way.' The advent of pulsestream economics coincided, not surprisingly, with a spate of early retirements in the business sector. Some 200 CEOs departed their companies between 2018 and 2028. There are almost certainly connections between Barrett and some of these executives, but their sheer number, coupled with a lack of post-Flare biographical data, makes any attempts at discovering their identities, as I have already noted elsewhere, a virtual impossibility.

[42] Assembling this book has not been without its pitfalls. I have encountered substantial gaps in documentation between the initial Hidden Wheel art show and the time of Stonecipher's record album was released, shortly before their only tour. Rather than reconstructing incidental events during this short period, I have chosen to allow Reese's journals to speak for themselves during the ill-documented interval.

[43] As a point of contrast, Barrett had already completed a canvas by this point.

[44] Initially, my thought was that Reese here refers to Gil Falcone, the frontman and only steady member of Dead Trend. After thorough investigation, I have discovered the Gil in question here is in fact Gil LaCorazza, whose impressive recording credentials include Blastfax's self-titled LP, and Terminal Harvest's well-regarded "Horizontal Lightning."

[45] Sic, I assume.

[46] The shift towards rapid, small communication methods that characterized the late 20th/early 21st century—from the aforementioned telephony to email to smaller bursts of quick information through such means as portable telephone and internet-based micromessaging—was seen as a constraint by some creative types, who took it upon themselves to intentionally misspell/misrepresent words as a means of self-expression.

[47] Highly publicized protests in Washington State at the turn of the century, rallying against loosening global trade regulations.

[48] Upwards of ten copies of "Center Ground," Melberg's fascinating study of Barrett and her work, still exist. I am grateful to the staff of the U.S. Library of Congress for their

patience and kindness towards me and my staff as we conducted our enlightening research on Melberg.

[49] Typically three syllables or less.

[50] The U.S. Library of Congress has one copy of Stonecipher's LP on file. None were found in Chicago, suggesting that Ms. Hotelier's hypothesis was false.

[51] The few surviving photos of Barrett, unavailable for reproduction because of the Barrett Trust's firm grip on all things Rhonda-related, portray her as a stunning beauty of radiance and grace undescribable by such a paltry talent as myself. Like her work itself, the photos must be seen to be believed.

[52] Reese's tour journal is strangely fragmented. These two passages, coupled with forthcoming entries on Boston and New York City, are all that were found in the Chicago vault.

The cities visited by Stonecipher on their tour boasted some of the most vibrant and interesting music of the late 20th and early 21st centuries. Based on the events detailed in both these entries and in the conclusion of this journal, it may be inferred that, whether through a lack of promotion or interest, the respective scene communities did not attend the band's shows. This strikes many historians, myself included, as particularly strange. Both Oxford Melberg and Cheryl Kearns have speculated that Amy Czjdeki's mood, based primarily on work-related anxiety, blackened over the course of the tour to the point where even well-attended, well-performed shows became inadequate. Both historians have valid points. The commonly accepted theory—that Czjdeki, burned out by many years of direct customer service at Conforti's restaurant and lulled into a false sense of importance by her time as Dead Trend's sixth bass player, felt entitled to a wider, higher-paying audience than Stonecipher's only tour was able to provide—is corroborated by her shift into restaurant management at the end of the tour. By leaving her position as a food server, Czjdeki effectively removed herself from close interactions with customers, shifting into a more administrative role. Kearns' "American Charge" details Czjdeki's rise to general manager at Conforti's, and her subsequent adoption of a child with eventual wife Rose Newtin.

It is interesting to note here that Reese's brief cohabitation with Rhonda Barrett came at a time which, with hindsight, seems wildly fortuitous when viewed in the light of Stonecipher's breakup. There are no indications in Reese's extant journals that Stonecipher was under any interpersonal duress. Quite to the contrary, the printed excerpts indicate that the band, flush with the success of recording, was at its interpersonal zenith, evidenced herein by Reese's complimentary descriptions of the band's sets. This scholar's opinion is that Reese's departure from the communal Nine Northbrook was an (un)happy accident, not a preemptive strike.

[53] The same low male voice heard during previous interviews, which I believe is that of Bernard Reese.

[54] Despite the profileration of the internet, broadcast radio remained a valuable resource for new and emerging bands before the AM and FM radio frequencies were purchased and reorganized by pulsestream providers. College stations, such as Freedom Springs University's station, unconstrained by the demands of ownership and/or advertising, played relatively unestablished bands

[55] Reese's geography is confused. The neighborhood adjacent to Boston University is Allston, not Cambridge.

[56] More than ten copies of Coxswain's vinyl debut still exist in private collections around the world.

[57] This interview passage, unlike the others, was transcribed. I remain unsure why Reese would write himself into the narrative as he does.

[58] The entire canvas is now illegible.

ADDITIONAL NOTES

I AM GRATEFUL TO THE U.S. Library of Congress for their assistance in this project. Rex Vineail assisted me in transferring the data on Bernard Reese's compact discs to a modern format. My colleagues at Freedom Springs University were supportive beyond measure. I thank you all.

The work of Amanda Hanson, Cheryl Kearns, Sidd Kraves and Oxford Melberg was instrumental in the production and arrangement of this work.

This work is in memory of the artists who made Freedom Springs so essential to the 21st century: Maxwell Caughin, Lara Fox-Turner, Bernard Reese, Benjamin Wilfork. And, of course, Rhonda Barrett.

THE FOLLOWING BITS OF EFFLUVIA are presented between chapters to add to the collage:

p. iv: Presumably from Seth Stina's collection, this is a flyer for an early Freedom Springs Dead Trend show. The exact start date of the band is lost to history, though their first, self-released demo tape indicates that some songs were written and recorded as early as May of 1986. It is unknown if other bands also played this bill.

p. 24: Also presumably from Stina's collection, this flyer is from one of Dead Trend's tours. 924 Gilman Street was an all-ages, collectively run non-profit punk club. I believe that, along with New York City's ABC No Rio and Worcester, Massachusetts' Space, Ben Wilfork loosely modeled Hidden Wheel around Gilman's organization.

P. 58: Max Caughin's graffiti tags, as 'Faze.' These appear to be from a sketchbook, where Caughin would have practiced his craft. Often, graffiti writers would draw small mock-ups of pieces later intended to be painted on walls, traincars, bridges, etc. in their sketchbooks. Sadly, no such drawings of Caughin's were ever found.

P. 80: Printouts of what are believed to be cityscapes on which Caughin based his CD case paintings. The blurriness and overall composition are consistent with descriptions of Caughin's work. The architecture depicted appears to be late nineteenth century. Buildings built in the period peppered Freedom Springs' financial district.

The angle of the photograph is consistent with Caughin's description of his later phase of work, when he took his photographs from a lower perspective.

P. 112: A flyer for a Festival of Hamburgers/Stonecipher show at Kensington, believed to be drawn by Katie Jackson, Festival's second guitarist. It's interesting to note that Coxswain's name has been left off this flyer, the omission likely fallout from Pee Valves' breakup. The misspelling of 'Stonecipher' indicates the relative newness of that band.

P. 126: Another flyer for the same show, likely created by Maddie Banks-Tingsen of Coxswain. We see no interpersonal animosity here. References to whaling and masted ships continued to be a motif throughout Coxswain's career.

P. 142: Another printout of what is likely the source material for Caughin's cityscapes. This photograph appears to have been taken earlier in Caughin's career, during the time he shot his photos in a more straight-ahead perspective.

P. 158: This photograph's players match the images of Dead Trend found in their first demo tape. From left to right: Mike Roft, guitar; Gil Falcone, vocals; Seth Stina, drums; Marty Harratt, bass. No date is listed/written on this photo, though I believe it to be from the 6/18/1986 Engelhardt Lounge show depicted in the flyer on page iv.

○ The Actual Credits

THANKS TO PETER CARLAFTES & KAT GEORGES of Three Rooms Press for their support and patience and pizza and everything else.

The porches of both Historic Three Wadsworth in Allston, Massachusetts (What up, Kevin!) and the Gideon Mayo House in Orono, Maine were crucial to this book's completion.

Dave Kress served as advisor to this book back when it was my MA thesis. It's safe to say that you wouldn't be reading without his suggestions and advice. Go get his books, available from Mammoth Press.

At the University of Maine, I read portions of this book, in various stages of completion, at the New Writing Series, spearheaded by Steve Evans and Jennifer Moxley. Pat Burnes and Jeff Evans offered kind suggestions while serving on my thesis committee. Tony Brinkley did the same over at the Franco-American Center.

Alex Irvine was nice enough to let me workshop this whole book in his fiction writing class. Jessica Putnam and Amanda Maxwell Updegraff had the good nature and patience to read it.

Bernie's interview with Richard Johnson first appeared, in different form, in The Accompanist, Megan London's Bangor-based literary journal. Similarly, passages from Hidden Wheel Art Gallery's opening first appeared in Stolen Island Review. Thank you!

Thanks to Tyler Babbie & Kate Kenderish, Katie Lattari, Joe Mayers & Lauren Weinbrown, Steve and Sarah Miller, Paige (and Lily) Mitchell, Adra Raine & Dave Harold, and Erin Workman & Kieran Daly for the Full Orono.

Tim Berrigan, Jay Grant and Mike Powers? That's a good policy. Shelly Fank took all the chapter break photos. You should see her puppets! Check www.shellyfank.com Ethan Dussault answered my questions about recording and production. He hopes my next book is about hockey. +1 Scene Point: Dr. Damian Adshead, Rachel, Benn & Mag at Atomic Books, Rob Bergen and Rachel Perry-Bergen, Don Bixtler, Boston Typewriter Orchestra, Bowery Poetry Club, Leslie Brokaw, Molly T. Bunny, Gwen Butler, Joe Carducci, Don Cheadle, Giordana and Peter Chipcagni, Coastwest Unrest, David Barker and Jean Mark Boling and everyone at Continuum Press, Marc "Gus" Desgroseilliers, Fluke Fanzine, Flywheel, Kristin Forbes, Michelle Fournier, all at Gargoyles On The Square, Pam Ginzler, Rob Gonella, Greasetrap, Great Western Plain, Travis Gowing, Joseph Grillo & Hilary Preston, Ned Greene & Eliza Burke-Greene, Wynne Gugliemo, Stan Hitron at Middlesex Community College, Ed Hochuli, Duncan Wilder Johnson, Dan Keezer, Kimmee & John LeBalmiero, Rich & Jackie Ladew-tang, Alvan Long, Gail Rush & all at New Alliance, Terry G. Lorber II & Lara Goodman, Mark Hanley, Zeth & Betsy Lundy (and their Central Street Farmhouse), Ed McNamara, Zeke Mermell, The Model Café, Honor Moody, Dale Nixon, Henry Owings and The Chunklet, Lisa Panepinto and Ryan Roderick, Scott Peterson, Pillowman, Rob Potylo, Q, Brendan Quigley and Liz Donovan, Wendy Raffel, Remember, Rideside, Saturday Jams, Dave Stoops and Cara DeBeer, Linda Sutherland at Emerson College, Nicole Tamarro, Tired Old Bones, Frank & Carrie Trippi, Meredith Turits, Wah-Tut-Ca Scout Reservation, Mike Watt, We Are Gong, WMEB, Woodman's, Christine Onorati @ Word, and You Go To Hell. Phew!

I'm fortunate to be surrounded by amazing family on all sides. Endless heaps of thanks to Anne and Lenny Boisclair, Dave and Sandi Griffin, Russ Griffin, Kathy and Jerry Lacroix, Tommy and Rachel Pichette, and the extended Boettcher/Fournier/Griffin/ Hebert/Melenke/Pichette/Stryna family, pets included.

This book—and all of 'em past and future—is dedicated to my parents, Ray and Kathy Fournier, for their unconditional love and support, and to my wife, Rebecca Griffin, for her good humor, patience, and understanding. I could not have done this without youse.

R.I.P.: Grace Fournier, Lance Hahn, Bruce W. Siart.

I'd love to read in your town/at your book club/with your band/at your school/etc. Hit me up:michaeltfournier@gmail.com

Michaeltfournier.tumblr.com and/or Deadtrend.bandcamp.com for more hoo-ha.

If you're not listed, I forgot to include your name, not you. That said, add it here: _____.

DALE NIXON

ABOUT THE AUTHOR

Michael T. Fournier's book-length discussion of the Minutemen's 1984 album "Double Nickels On The Dime" is the 45th installment of Continuum Press's "33 1/3" series. His writing has appeared in Pennsylvania English, Stolen Island Review, Pitchfork, Fluke, Chunklet and the Boston Phoenix. He has taught literature and punk rock history at Emerson College, Tufts University and University of Maine. He lives in Western Massachusetts with his wife Rebecca and their cat.

books on **three rooms press**

POETRY

by Peter Carlaftes
DrunkYard Dog
I Fold with the Hand I Was Dealt

by Ryan Buynak
Yo Quiero Mas Sangre

by Joie Cook
When Night Salutes the Dawn

by Thomas Fucaloro
Inheriting Craziness is
   Like a Soft Halo of Light

by Kat Georges
Our Lady of the Hunger
Punk Rock Journal

by Karen Hildebrand
One Foot Out the Door
Take a Shot at Love

by Matthew Hupert
Ism is a Retrovirus

by Dominique Lowell
Sit Yr Ass Down or You Ain't
   gettin no Burger King

by B. R. Lyon
You Are White Inside

by Jane Ormerod
Recreational Vehicles on Fire

by Susan Scutti
We Are Related

by Jackie Sheeler
to[o] long

by The Bass Player from Hand Job
Splitting Hairs

by Angelo Verga
Praise for What Remains

by George Wallace
Poppin' Johnny

PLAYS

by Madeline Artenberg &
Karen Hildebrand
The Old In-and-Out

by Peter Carlaftes
Triumph For Rent (3 Plays)
Teatrophy (3 More Plays)

by Larry Myers
Mary Anderson's Encore
Twitter Theater

HUMOR

by Peter Carlaftes
A Year on Facebook

PHOTOGRAPHY-MEMOIR

by Mike Watt
On & Off Bass

FICTO-MEMOIR

by Ronnie Norpel
Baseball Karma & The
   Constitution Blues

FICTION

by Michael T. Fournier
Hidden Wheel

ANTHOLOGIES / JOURNALS

Maintenant
Journal of Contemporary Dada Art
& Literature (annually since 2003)

Have a NYC
Tall Tales from The City

three rooms press
new york, ny | www.threeroomspress.com

CPSIA information can be obtained at www.ICGtesting.com
Printed in the USA
BVOW012253240112

281310BV00001B/4/P